Alien Encounters...

"Have you gotten any more information?" Boelling asked.

"None of them can talk."

"Their tongues?"

"In part that, but they've all undergone a tremendous shock. They may never come back."

"What, exactly? All I've heard is that they've been cut up pretty bad."

"Cut *on* is more like it. Dissected. I think you'd better have a look, doctor."

THE ADAM EXPERIMENT

The near-future thriller by
GEOFFREN SIMMONS

THE ADAM EXPERIMENT

A NOVEL BY GEOFFREY SIMMONS

A BERKLEY BOOK
published by
BERKLEY PUBLISHING CORPORATION

This Berkley book contains the complete
text of the original hardcover edition.
It has been completely reset in a type face
designed for easy reading, and was printed
from new film.

THE ADAM EXPERIMENT

A Berkley Book / published by arrangement with
Arbor House Publishing Company, Inc.

PRINTING HISTORY
Arbor House edition published 1978
Berkley edition / October 1979

ISBN: 0-425-04492-0

A BERKLEY BOOK ® TM 757,375
Berkley Books are published by Berkley Publishing Corporation,
200 Madison Avenue, New York, New York 10016.
PRINTED IN THE UNITED STATES OF AMERICA

FOR CATHY AND BRADLEY

Prologue

Man has always been interested in conquering new lands and seeking out areas that no one has ever been to before. This challenge of the unknown antedates written history and although economic needs were among the inciting motives, just the mere desire to be first and see what lies one step beyond was enough to drive some men. So it was with much of the early space exploration. In particular, the Pioneer probes. Originally, their goal was to reach the moon, just to see what was there and say that they did it. Later, it became the stars and with the change, a need to tell whoever and whatever was out there that we also existed.

Like most scientific endeavors, the early stages of the Pioneer space program had their variety of errors—mechanical and human—but the last two stages, Pioneer X and XI, contained the seed of cosmic presumption—man's first small step toward extinction?

On October 11, 1958, Pioneer I was launched. It reached an altitude of 70,000 miles on top of a Thor-Able rocket and then fell silently back to earth the next day.

Four weeks later, a similar attempt was made with Pioneer II, but the third stage of the launch rocket failed and the satellite plummeted back.

On December 6, 1958, a much smaller version, Pioneer III, weighing thirteen pounds, was launched on top of a Juno rocket. It, too, died prematurely, barely reaching 64,000 miles.

Four months later came Pioneer IV, a moderate success by comparison. It was launched in March of 1959 and managed to pass within 37,000 miles of the moon.

Unfortunately, it too was aimed directly at the lunar surface.

An identical attempt followed eight months later which failed as the payload shroud broke away at lift-off. Because of the failure, this attempt was never given a number.

During the early sixties, the program changed. With the development of the Ranger crash-landing camera vehicles, the Pioneers were switched to deep space exploration instead.

On March 11, 1960, Pioneer V reached 22.5 million miles and went into a solar orbit. This was followed in 1965 with Pioneer VI, in 1966 with Pioneer VII, in 1967 with Pioneer VIII, and in 1968 with Pioneer IX, all hurled out into elliptical orbits around the sun. A Delta rocket was used this time and with major improvements in construction, new materials and additional shielding the satellite's longevity was extended from a few months to several years.

By the 1970's, NASA was ready for even deeper probes, and on March 3, 1972, Pioneer X was launched from Cape Kennedy on top of an Atlas-Centaur rocket. Its objectives were to explore the interplanetary medium beyond Mars, to investigate the Asteroid Belt between Mars and Jupiter, to determine its navigability, and to explore the surface of Jupiter in a "fly-by" orbit. If it then were able to escape Jupiter's gravity, it would proceed onward into outer space.

As part of its scientific equipment, it carried a message from earth in the form of a gold-anodized aluminum plaque that was engraved with the images of a nude man and woman poised against the outline of the satellite itself and a complicated pulsar diagram that showed where the satellite originated—the third planet of the solar system.

It was an engraved invitation, with directions included.

THE ADAM EXPERIMENT

The Beginning

I

October 29, 1991

As THE graveyard shift at Mission Control approached the seven A.M. changeover, the satellite communications section was quiet. To the skeleton crew on duty, it had been a typical, uneventful night—nothing out of the ordinary had happened and nothing was expected. Among the dozens of consoles usually in use, only a few were lit up and most of them were geared to monitoring signals from Space Labs IV and V. Thus far, all systems in each were working well. They had been for months.

Seated alone toward the back was Sergeant Lester Stevens, a heavy set man in his early forties who made constant use of coffee to keep himself alert. It always had to be hot and black. In front of him, a console screen kept repeating a long series of numbers, all frequencies for ancillary communication links with a variety of less important satellites. In a way, he was the back-up man as these were also emergency channels if anything went wrong.

It was a relatively easy assignment, more tedious than anything else. While he watched, the computer did most of his work and whenever a radio signal was received, usually from a weather probe with mechanical problems, the computer would automatically switch to the appropriate channel and type out the message. Sometimes it was coded and sometimes not, depending on the satellite's classification, but it didn't matter to Stevens. He knew most of the codes by heart and his job essentially boiled down to tearing off the terminal sheet, retrieving the description folder, and delivering them both to the commanding officer.

As Stevens tossed his empty Styrofoam cup into an automatic disposal slot and put on his jacket to leave, the scanner light abruptly stopped midway across the panel and a moment later, the terminal keys below were rapidly firing away. Although it was the change of shift and he could easily turn the message over to his replacement who had just arrived, curiosity kept him there instead. It was the communique's channel that caught his attention. It was one that he'd never seen used before.

z901-4y11007788
TIME: 0700
TERMINATION SIGNAL RECEIVED FROM
PIONEER X.

"Termination signal?" Stevens reacted with surprise. "That can't be." As far as he knew none of the satellites in use had a built in termination signal. Their radio signals merely faded and then were lost. In addition, the Pioneer program had been dead for years and if Pioneer X was even functioning, which he doubted, it had to be billions of miles away. Convinced that a mistake had been made, he quickly pushed the recheck button, but a moment later, the computer's memory bank confirmed the message and the source. Pioneers X and XI were the only two satellites that had ever used the Z901 frequency.

"That's impossible," Stevens insisted as if he were arguing with the computer and then showed the readout sheet to his replacement.

"Maybe it's some monster from outer space." The man joked, obviously not as concerned.

"Something's gone screwy. That's for sure," Stevens said with a forced smile. "I think I'll check this one out myself." He gathered up the sheet and his other papers and immediately headed toward the file room.

The files were located five floors below in an underground vault—a security clearance on his level, a locked elevator down, another security clearance as he exited and an electronic pass to enter the steel vault. Everything pertinent to the space exploration program was stored there, beginning with information garnered from the German rocket experiments during World War II through the Viking and Apollo attempts, the space shuttle work and the Space Labs, covering everything from top secret computer tapes of the various rocket machinery to plumbing and recreational plans on the larger satellites. Nothing was thrown out. Every piece of scratch paper, every memo, every computer calculation was saved.

The Pioneer files were located toward the back, relegated to the archives where they served more as historical background than any useful purpose in present day research. In space exploration, the 1950's and 1960's were ancient history, the Indian hunting canoe in an age of ocean liners. The information on Jupiter and Saturn had been updated and totally revised and the information on the outer rim of the solar galaxy was too gross to even consider.

The data on Pioneer X occupied an entire file cabinet, four deep drawers, much of whose information was microfilmed or on computer tape. After finally locating the original manual on the launching protocol, Stevens began thumbing through in search of communication channels. He was trying to confirm that a termination signal didn't exist—he was sure of it—but he was soon astonished to see that he was mistaken. Under the last paragraph he found:

> "In the event that the satellite's external seal is ever broken and the scientific equipment inside is either tampered with or removed, a termination signal will be transmitted to Mission Control along frequency Z901."

Before
The Beginning

II

IF ONE can date the origin of any experiment, the Ceres project, named after the first asteroid discovered and the mythical goddess of fertility, probably began six months previously when Dr. Harold Olmschied, an aging medical geneticist, had flown to Washington. He was on his way to see the Financial Director of the Space Commission, Lawrence O'Hara, a man whom he'd been trying to call for days and had now decided to confront personally.

Although it was springtime in the capital, the air was still nippy and as Olmschied exited his taxi and started up the steps, he was bundled up in a heavy woolen coat, a long blue scarf, and a weathered fedora. Beneath the skirts of his coat, he walked with a limp. It wasn't enough to hobble him or require a cane, but the pain in his right knee was apparent with every other step, always making him shift his weight to the healthier leg. His hair was silver gray with a crown of white beneath the hat's brim, his mustache peppery and there were deep furrows across his forehead. He looked serious.

Halfway up the twenty-six steps, he stopped for a breather, switched his briefcase to the other hand and glanced upward at the remaining climb. Within his chest he could feel his heart struggling—a skipped beat, three normal beats and then another pause. After cursing the architect responsible for his dilemma, he took a deep breath and proceeded on. If you want money, he thought, you have to work for it. So far, his newest proposal had been rejected for petty, nonsensical reasons, and he was determined to get financial support if he had to stay in O'Hara's office all night.

Once he reached the top landing, he felt exhilarated. Senior citizen conquers Mt. Everest, he thought wryly. Not only conquers it, but survives the assault. After popping a nitroglycerin tablet under his tongue to quiet the gnawing pain in his chest, he continued. The medication always gave him a headache, but it also meant it was working. Without it, he'd probably have had a dozen heart attacks by now.

The electric doors in front of the building parted as he approached, waited patiently for him to pass through, and then quickly closed with a swishing sound behind him. A second set then opened and closed in the same manner. Beyond were two guards seated at a desk with a series of television screens in front of them.

"Can I help you?" One of the guards asked in a matter-of-fact but polite tone.

"No help needed." He didn't have the time or patience to play their security games. They should know who he was. He'd been here a dozen times before, didn't need their help to find his way.

The guard, however, was required to stop everyone who entered, including employees whom he personally recognized. Saboteurs had gone to extraordinary ends to disguise themselves, including plastic surgery, and now everyone without exception had to pass through a security check.

"Sorry, sir," he said, sounding more annoyed with Olmschied's attitude than apologetic for the inconvenience, and then automatically locked the next succession of doors. Beside him, the other guard unlatched his revolver holster. "Your name and destination, please."

"Mr. O'Hara knows that I'm coming," Olmschied said, pushing against the frozen doors.

"Your name, sir."

"Olmschied . . . Dr. Harold Olmschied."

The guard proceeded to punch in O'Hara's identification number and then added the professor's name. A moment later, the screen confirmed their appointment at 1:45 and added a picture with data.

Olmschied, Harold S., M.D., Ph.D.
Age: 72
Ht: 5'6"

Wt: 150 Pounds
Hair: gray
Eyes: hazel
Race: caucasian
Complexion: fair
Dist. marks: mole on right cheek, scar in right eyebrow

The second guard asked him to place both hands on a transparent plate at the edge of their desk. Reluctantly, Olmschied complied. After his clothes were searched for concealed weapons, his briefcase was channeled through an X-ray monitoring device. Only books and papers could be seen inside, and once considered safe, he was allowed to proceed. No apologies for the inconvenience was made. They never were.

Director O'Hara's office was located on the eighth floor and at the end of a long, carpeted corridor. As the professor entered the suite, he was surprised to see that there had been a change in secretaries. Instead of the matronly, often sympathetic Mrs. Hastings, who had quietly helped him in the past, he found himself confronting a platinum blonde with glossy red lipstick and a deep cleavage beneath her sheer blouse.

"What happened to Mrs. Hastings?" Olmschied asked as he hung his coat on a hanger. He had hoped to gain some last minute insight into their rejection.

"She's no longer with us. Retirement rules, you know. She was fifty-five last week. Retirement's mandatory at fifty-five for anyone in civil service, you know...."

He didn't.

In the next room over, Director O'Hara had already braced himself with a double scotch for their meeting. The balding director usually waited until after four to start his drinking, a habit he blamed on the pressures of his position, but today he made an exception. He could have refused to see the professor, found some excuse, but knew that it would look bad and probably only intensify the professor's outrage. Olmschied had too many friends, and although most were old and retiring, they were still influential. There was also the news media. If word got out that he had crudely turned away the world famous geneticist, he'd have some embarrassing explanations to make. No, he had to see him, even if it took two doubles.

In a way, he liked the old man, at least from a distance. He considered him one of the more brilliant scientists around, but couldn't take his unreasoning stubbornness. Conversation with him was often one sided, like an old schoolmaster who insisted on the exact adherence to a set of arbitrary rules which he alone established and felt were God given. Olmschied rarely listened to departmental recommendations, frequently rejected criticism, constructive or other, and never followed the rules. That is, unless he made them.

The problem today was not so much his work as his health. He was getting old. Retirement rules didn't apply to the scientific community, but aerospace research was shifting from the ground level to the Space Labs and members of the Space Commission Board thought that the professor was too far along to make the adjustment. They wanted younger scientists who could endure prolonged space travel and the inherent risks. Much of the future space work depended on it and obviously, Olmschied didn't fit the image. Taking him along not only represented a risk to his health, but to his work as well. There was always the possibility that a vital part of his experiments might end prematurely, and at the costs of aerospace research the dollar figure was inhibiting. Instead they were willing to offer him one of the less important positions at ground level, and it had become O'Hara's job to convince the man to take one. It was a chore he'd been dreading for weeks.

As Olmschied marched into the director's office, he already had his briefcase open and by the time he reached the desk there was a thick packet of papers tightly gripped in his hand. Without a word he set the pile down in front of O'Hara, then retrieved a second set equally voluminous.

"What's all this?" O'Hara said.

"Proof. Proof that Gregor's experiment can't succeed and mine can." He was referring to Professor Conrad Gregor's work at Stanford on the use of artificial hibernation in space travel. The two men had angrily debated the method for years.

"It's already been shown to work."

"Here on earth, perhaps, but it's far too dangerous for trips beyond the solar system. To master the universe, man must reproduce as he has already done to conquer his own world. The thirteen colonies would never have survived if the Pilgrims had come here as frozen mummies. The challenge is met in numbers, not ice cubes. If man sleeps en route, who knows what he'll miss. Just between Denver and Los Angeles that could mean the Grand Canyon. Who knows what emergencies might come up and not leave time for some astronaut to defrost. No, he must remain awake for the entire journey, and we must proceed to demonstrate that procreation in space is possible."

"I'm sure that the Commission has that in mind for the future—"

"I doubt it, or they would have granted *me* laboratory space, not him."

"We can't have people fornicating on the Space Lab just to prove your point, you know. And besides, you've already shown that conception is safe with rats—"

"Rats aren't human beings, surely you've noticed that. What's true of apples isn't necessarily true of oranges and grapefruits even though they all grow on trees. The next step is monkeys. They're a much closer relative—"

"I don't think it's possible..." O'Hara started to explain the Commission's concern over his health, then hesitated. In spite of the nights without sleep, he still didn't know how to say it.

"Of course it's possible and I know you still have room on the Lab." His information had come from Mrs. Hastings a few weeks before and he was hoping that he was still right, which was what he'd planned to ask her.

O'Hara was surprised that he knew about the available space, although it was only one small laboratory. He had considered lying about the Lab being full, but now he was cornered and decided to let out the real reason. "The Commission doesn't think that your health can handle it." "Health" was a good choice of words, he thought. Better than "age," at least.

"Nonsense. Conditions without gravity would be an improvement for my legs."

"And what about your heart?"

The question momentarily stunned Olmschied. His physical impairment was obvious, but he'd thought that his heart condition was a secret.

"We have to keep up on the health of everyone who works for the Commission. I'm sorry."

Olmschied was silent for a minute. He'd compromise. "Then I'll take an associate, someone whose health you can absolutely depend on and so be confident work will go on."

"I don't know . . . space is limited, time is short, I'll have to take it up with the Board . . . it's really their decision anyway. But who did you have in mind?"

"Dr. Cortney Miles." Olmschied pulled out the name of one of his previous graduate students. This was the first time that he'd given any thought to using an associate, and her name was the first to come to mind. It was a good choice nonetheless, he thought. She was conscientious, intelligent, well-qualified and certain to make a good impression on the Board.

The name Miles didn't ring a bell with the Director, but he conceded that Olmschied's proposal was a possible alternative. After requesting a dossier on this associate, he said he'd give the professor an answer in a month. If it was still no then, at least he had some time to come up with a better way to handle him.

III

THE PRESSURES of a divorce hearing could probably never compare to those of performing open heart surgery, but they were enough and it was over and he could get his mind back on his work... or so thought Dr. John Hicks as he left the courthouse and headed back toward Michael Reese Hospital. She had been excised from his life, removed, legally and physically. As he stopped his car at the first traffic light, he loosened his tie, unbuttoned the top of his shirt, pushed his dark hair back from his forehead and managed to smile at himself in the rearview mirror. This was the first time that he had felt human in weeks.

The divorce had been uncontested, a ten-year marriage that had ended on a note of adultery—hers, but he was still forced to hang his wash out for everyone to see. No way to prevent it. Anything short of another man, he might not have left Marilyn, but visions of coming home early one day and finding her in bed with someone else... his bed, his wife, his home, all in disarray without an apparent damn for his feelings... that hurt the most. Once, hard to believe, he had loved everything about her. Now, face it, there was none of it left.

Fortunately there weren't any children, though it wasn't from his lack of trying. Marilyn's modeling career didn't accommodate stretch marks, they'd show up on photographs like dents on a used car; not to mention her breasts might dangerously sag, and with them lucrative job offers. Once, fed up, he accused her of trimming her pubic hair more often than he shaved. Not a pretty phrase, and he wasn't too proud of himself for saying it... well, now he was rid of all that wrangling... they both were...

Although he hadn't given much thought to it in the past, suddenly the notion of being a bachelor again was rather tantalizing. Women, parties, booze? No, that wasn't really his way, but at least he could live his life as he wanted and he could seek out other relationships without any feeling of guilt. Marriage was out, though. He'd just had enough. Mrs. Right could come along and he probably wouldn't give her a second look, or even recognize her.

The thirty-two-year-old surgeon belonged to a nationally known heart team at the University of Chicago Medical School. His Chief was Dr. Leonard Baumeister, the inventor of the artificial heart and whose breakthrough discovery seven years earlier had won him the Nobel prize. Ever since, the department had been inundated with requests to help ailing patients around the world.

Much like Dr. Christiaan Barnard years before, fortuitous circumstances had made Baumeister first. Three other surgical teams were waiting at the same time to try out their device, but Baumeister happened to get the right patient at the right time.

The subject was a teenage boy who was crushed in a train-car accident when his VW stalled on the tracks. By the time the paramedics were able to free his body he was in shock and his heart was irreparably damaged. The electrical tracing was normal, but the heart just didn't have enough strength to pump his blood around. Pressure readings were zero over zero while his heart rate raced at 220 beats a minute to compensate. Cardiopulmonary resuscitation was begun and maintained during transport to Michael Reese Hospital, where it was shown that the heart wall had been badly lacerated.

By coincidence, Dr. Baumeister's team was just closing another case upstairs and when the call came, they quickly shifted to the operating room next door. Six hours later, the first mechanical heart was installed and by the twentieth hour the boy was taken off the critical list. The accomplishment was enough to put Baumeister's name in the history books along with Salk, Fleming and Pasteur. A second team at Cedars-Sinai in Los Angeles followed up with a similar case two days later, but in medicine there has never been a win, place, and show.

It was precisely that winning reputation of Baumeister's that made Hicks apply to the University's residency program. Having graduated first in his class at Harvard and won honors in all six categories of the National Boards, any door would have gladly opened to him, but he only wanted one. Baumeister's. If you can have the best, why settle for anything less.

During his first two years on staff he was low man on the totem pole, the fraternity pledge. There was a definite pecking order, determined mostly by seniority, and the most responsibility given to him was being second assistant. He was there to help and to learn by observation, not by doing. He would stand for hours holding retractors until he felt as though he'd pass out from immobility and then, in the end, a bone for being good, they'd allow him to sew up the skin. Had he gone to a county hospital, he'd already be doing some of the technical work, but here he was among some of the country's best, each a prima donna, and he had to wait his turn. By the third year he'd moved up to first assistant (a new resident took over as second), and his natural abilities began to shine. By his fourth year it was apparent that he was destined to become a skillful surgeon, and even Dr. Baumeister, the master, liked what he saw. Soon Hicks became his personal assistant and not unexpectedly, when it came to his last year, he was asked to stay on at the University....

After parking his car in the doctor's lot, Hicks readjusted his tie. Although his O.R. cases were covered for the day, he still had to finish up some paperwork and plan the next day's schedule: two mechanical hearts, a lung transplant, and a nuclear pacemaker. It was all routine—six hours of work if all went well, eight if not.

As he entered the hospital lobby and headed toward the elevators, an attractive receptionist in the administrator's office glanced his way. Blue eyes, a friendly smile. Although he'd seen her before this was the first time he'd actually looked, and he liked what he saw. He made a mental note to come back and proceeded on.

When he arrived in his office, he found a note from Baumeister. "Call as soon as you get in!" An exclamation point meant important. Using the videophone, he punched a two digit number and waited.

A few seconds later, the chief surgeon's face was on the screen, robust with rosy cheeks, wire rimmed glasses and a smile. Baumeister always smiled, even in the face of tragedy.

"John, you're finally back. I trust everything went all right?"

Hicks shrugged his shoulders. "It went as I expected." He really didn't want to talk about it. "You wanted me to call?"

"Are you going to be there for a minute or two?"

"Sure, but I can come up there."

"No, that won't be necessary. I'll be right down."

The screen went dark and less than a minute later Baumeister was entering his office.

"It must be awfully important to get you to move that quickly," Hicks said. "What movie star or senator we getting this time?"

Baumeister carefully closed the door behind him, and waited until he was seated to speak. "Something better." He paused. "Something much better. A trip to Space Lab V."

"The Space Lab?"

"Absolutely. I proposed a project last year. I didn't really think that they'd take us, but I received confirmation from the Space Commission today. One million dollars worth. We leave in two months."

"We leave? Part of 'we' doesn't know anything about this. I expected to be moving out of my house, not half way to the sun—"

"I couldn't tell you until now. Competition, you know. Someone else gets wind of it, underbids me and it's gone. Not that I didn't trust you, but I didn't want anyone to know about it until we got approved. It's all simple stuff anyway. You don't need to prepare a thing. Just pack. It's the same dog surgery we do around here for practice, only this time, it'll be under weightless conditions."

It wasn't appropriate to ask someone of Baumeister's stature if he'd lost their marbles, but for once Hicks was tempted. "Isn't heart surgery a little premature? Nothing more complicated than removing a splinter has been done in outer space before."

"A virgin field. Perfect for us."

"But why heart. Why didn't the Commission go for abdominal exploration or pinning hips?"

"What's the most injurious part of our work? What above all other things, including infection, hinders us?"

"The heart's constant motion." He felt like a pupil again. The answer was common knowledge. Unlike all other bodily organs or tissues that could be bandaged or splinted during the healing process, the heart, for obvious reasons, had to remain in constant motion.

"Precisely. But what if the heart suddenly didn't have to work so hard? What if it didn't have to fight at all? During rest, the measured heart rates in astronauts is known to fall off fifty percent. Sometimes more. Oxygen consumption is down. Basic metabolism is reduced."

"In other words, we fly up there with a bunch of dogs, open their hearts, and then see how quickly they heal?"

Baumeister's face lit up. "Exactly. What do you think?"

Hicks hesitated for only a moment. It was a delicious challenge, an opportunity he couldn't resist, and certainly a chance to get away from it all.

IV

By 0720, Sergeant Stevens was in General Boelling's office with the teletype sheet in one hand and Pioneer folders in the other. At the moment the commanding officer, a tall lanky man with graying temples, was just arriving and hurriedly gathering classified documents for a staff meeting. He appeared to be running late and annoyed at the interruption.

"Can't it wait?" he asked, pulling a set of keys from his pocket and unlocking a cabinet drawer.

"I received a message this morning that I think you'd better take a look at," Stevens said, setting the sheet down on the desk in front of Boelling.

The general closed the cabinet drawer and stepped closer. As he read the words, his expression changed from annoyance to confusion. "Termination signal? What termination signal?"

Stevens handed him the relevant sheets from the folder and waited. The paragraph under Communications was self-explanatory.

"Are you sure about this?"

"Double-checked it."

"There must be a mistake."

"I don't think so."

Boelling flipped on his intercom and told his secretary to cancel the day's meeting. He wanted Dr. Harold Leigh at the Space Commission. The professor was director of operations and his immediate supervisor. If the message meant what he thought it did . . .

Dr. Leigh was out of his office and it took his secretary several minutes to locate him. As he sat down in front of the videoscreen, he appeared to be out of breath. "What's up?" It was his favorite bad pun.

Boelling relayed what they'd received and the explanation found in the files. The professor was silent for a moment. No more jokes.

"Any chance there's a mistake?"

"Not from what I gather."

Leigh was silent again.

"It does seem strange that we'd hear after all these years."

The professor nodded. "I'll get back to you. I think we'd better take this to the full Commission right away. I think the White House ought to know too."

After the screen went blank, Boelling relocked his files and followed Stevens back to his station. He had to double-check the message himself.

V

IT WAS exactly 0900 when General Lyndquist began making his inspection rounds on Space Lab V. In another hour the first group of researchers would be docking in their shuttle flight and he wanted to be certain that everything was in good order before they arrived. He had already checked out the research section the night before, but the blond-haired, fifty-year-old commander was meticulous, organized, ready. This morning he had dispensed with the customary nylon suit and was wearing his Air Force uniform instead.

During the previous two months more than twenty million dollars in scientific equipment had arrived from Kennedy and Houston. At first the flights came weekly, but as the July deadline approached, the shuttles were stepped up to every other day. Each ship had limited space and Mission Control was determined to start on time, no matter what the cost. Delays now only meant additional costs later.

In a way, the giant satellite was an experiment in itself, hovering three hundred thousand miles out and following the earth in its elliptical orbit around the sun, but its actual purpose was now only beginning. Here, man would finally have the opportunity to assess all measurable aspects of life in outer space, lay the groundwork for deeper probes that were certain to follow and try out the newest equipment under actual conditions. It was an ideal laboratory setting and much of future space exploration depended on its work. Lyndquist was the satellite's first commander, and proud of it.

Space Lab V, or the Flying Saucer as it was known by the three-thousand-man crew, was built in the shape of a gigantic disk, fifty feet deep and a half mile across. In the center was a spherical structure making the ship itself seem like a miniaturized replica of the planet Saturn on end. It spun at a rate of one revolution per minute, thereby creating a centrifugal force along the outer rim that mimicked earth's own gravity. Inside, a man could start walking at one point, believe that he was traveling in a straight line, and actually make a full circle over-head. His only clue that his body's orientation might be changing would be the slight incline in the distant corridor, but the change was so imperceptible that few people ever gave it much thought. Upside down, sideways or even backwards in outer space was usually irrelevant.

The same centrifugal force was lost when one traveled toward the central core or "hub." Here, within the confines of a metal eggshell, was where most of the research work would be done. Other than its dependence on the main unit for oxygen and the external shielding against cosmic radiation, the five-story research unit was identical to conditions just beyond its walls. Scientists could live along the rim at night under conditions that simulated life on earth and yet work during the daytime hours under weightless laboratory conditions that were only a short elevator ride away.

The east elevator, named only for convenience sake, was nearest to Lyndquist's quarters, and as he entered it now he added the Velcro sandals to his boots. At normal gravity their tenacious grip was a definite hindrance, but once beyond the 0.5 gravity mark (half way to the hub), they were necessary to keep one's balance.

Lyndquist pushed the button for central core, then listened to a woman's voice instruct him to take a seat and fasten himself in. A barely audible purring sound followed as the tiny cubicle began to accelerate inward.

Altogether there were four separate elevator shafts located equal distance apart along the outer rim. In each, the ride toward the center seemed upward but it was really a matter of perspective. In actuality the passenger either rode toward or away from the gravity source and once inside the hub had to change his bearings to a completely different local vertical that was perpendicular to the plane of the satellite. A man standing in the outer rim was at right angles to a man standing in the laboratories.

Space Lab V was Lyndquist's baby. His own mansion, built on unlimited acreage and costing well over four billion dollars. He had been there since its inception, helping weld the first aluminum panels together and later supervising three hundred men during its assemblage, all prefabricated materials brought from earth. In those days he felt more like a construction engineer than an aerospace commander. Electricians, plumbers, carpenters, all designated with the prefix "astro-" were there. Only the architects remained back on earth.

The Space Lab projects had evolved in much the same manner as the Pioneers and Vikings. Each was an improvement over its predecessor; each orbiting a bit further out into space. Now Island I was scheduled to be the Space Commission's next step. Although the mammoth project was still on the drawing boards, it was conceived to be the biggest, most challenging yet. Within its confines a town of fifteen thousand people would live as they might on earth with all the accouterments: restaurants, movies, barbershops, department stores, parks, a hospital, its own farms and its own industries—man's first true attempt at colonization.

Lyndquist's ship, as well as Island I, owed their financing to the success of Space Lab IV whose accomplishments had exceeded everyone's expectations, including the Space Commission's. Originally it had been designed to help relieve the energy crisis on earth, but instead it was able to harvest enough solar energy to support the entire nation's needs. The giant satellite looked like a huge, multicolored butterfly with wings of solar cells that stretched twenty miles across and ten miles in length. Far beneath, four receiving stations in the Rockies and three others in the Appalachians converted the microwave relay to electricity. Once fully functional, the ship's daily output was enough to service a city of a million.

At the time of Space Lab IV's construction, 1988, the energy crunch was severe. The fears of the 1970's had suddenly become reality: Arab oil depleted, multiple nuclear accidents, curtailed fusion work and too much pollution from coal usage. Solar resuscitation returned perspectives to normal again and with it, space projects were once again easily funded.

Construction work on Space Lab V began the following year—1989. The beginning nucleus was a hull from an old Skylab that was merely jettisoned further out into space. At first it was barely large enough to support four men, but as the satellite grew so did room for additional crew. The teams worked twelve-hour shifts, seven days a week and rotated a week of leave on earth every three months. Prolonged weightlessness had its hazards and the Space Commission insisted on that single week back in their normal environment.

The skeleton was built first, four elevator shafts that stretched out from the center like spokes in a wheel. Then, like tiny spiders, they began filling in the spaces with their metallic web. The inner circles were done in a matter of days, but as they expanded outward, their progress slowed, needing three months to close the outer rim. Even after the installation of the last panel another six months was still required to complete the interior, and then several more weeks of testing. Lyndquist presided over every minute of it.

As his elevator now ascended toward zero gravity, his feet were plastered to the floor but it was a deceptive feeling. Once the elevator slowed, it was only his seat belt and Velcro soles that kept him from being thrown to the ceiling. The door opened and the same woman's voice announced that he was entering the central core, that he was now weightless and that the local vertical was to the right. The floor was now the wall, and he climbed downward to regain the proper orientation.

Once outside, the commander's husky body moved gracefully through the empty corridor as if he had suddenly been converted to slow motion. A few loose papers floated up from his coat pocket, but he quickly retrieved them and placed them in a more secure place. His eyes studied everything. The Velcro carpeting, the shiny metal walls, the direction signs, the open hatchways. There were no stairs or elevators, only ladders which were easy for a single man to pass through but cramped for some of the scientific equipment. Compensating for the difficulty was their lack of weight. Half-ton computers were lifted with foolish ease.

Lyndquist slowly climbed to the fourth level and began checking the cartons for their color codes. Four was orange, Dr. Gregor's section, and his name was boldly printed on the sides of his cartons. Next he moved to the fifth level, the red section, and the names here were Baumeister and Olmschied. He was familiar with both names and excited about meeting them. Dr. Gregor's work with frozen bodies struck him as rather ghoulish—a personal feeling that he never openly expressed. Well, the Stanford professor's work was something that he'd just have to tolerate.

Located above the fifth level was one of the ship's two crow's nests—their visual lookout station designed to compliment and aid the electronic surveillance equipment inside the command post at the rim. On duty was Corporal Emil Kreuger, a double-leg amputee who'd been with Lyndquist from the beginning. Here, he was in his ideal milieu. The combined effect of weightlessness and limited space had made him much more maneuverable than other crewmen and instead of being handicapped, he was at a distinct advantage.

"Anything?" Lyndquist asked as he stuck his head through the hatchway and found himself looking straight up at Kreuger high in the plastic bubble.

"Just some fly-bys. The largest wasn't any bigger than a pea. Too small to shoot at." Kreuger sounded disappointed, then changed his tone. "There's your shuttle flight." He pointed toward the winged ship coming from earth's direction.

The commander nodded and pushed himself further inside to get a better look.

"I guess it's going to be a little crowded around here with everyone working in the laboratories," Kreuger said. So far, he'd enjoyed the quiet and solitude.

"Crowded's probably not the only thing. The most preparation anyone in that group's had is two weeks, and it's all been through books and tapes."

"Two weeks?" Kreuger thought back on the six-month ordeal he'd undergone.

"The Commission wants us to break everyone in. They say it's more practical up here, but I'm not so sure."

Kreuger eyed the approaching shuttle again, and although he agreed with Lyndquist, he knew it really wasn't his problem.

The intercom interrupted to announce that the shuttle would be docking in twenty minutes. Lyndquist realized time was short and quickly descended to the second and first levels, the middle being only a central corridor. . . .

Originally Lyndquist had been trained as a fighter pilot. He was a graduate of the Air Force Academy with a master's degree in aeronautical engineering, but that was the peaceful 1980's. The surfeit of pilots, primarily due to the advent of cruise missiles, caused many to be shifted to the aerospace program. Lyndquist was one of them and ten months later he was on board Apollo XV traveling toward Mars.

The trip took three months each way. Lyndquist was the second pilot (the customary crew was two pilots and a navigator). When they arrived, the protocol called for the other two men to explore the surface for mining sites while he remained behind in case of trouble, which no one expected.

It came when the other two mistakenly set their exploring vehicle down along the rim of a crater they presumed to be a meteor's indentation but was in fact the summit caldera of an active volcano. Literally before they knew it, the heat from the lava beds had melted their rockets and they were being sucked downward into a bath of boiling quicksand. Their distress calls became screams. All systems were failing, and if the rising temperature inside their cabin didn't kill them, the ship's oxygen tanks were certain to explode.

Regulations were clear: "No attempts at dangerous recoveries are to be made." Everyone who entered the astronaut program knew this. To expose a third man and his ship to an equal calamity was against the rules. If possible, someone from the crew had to report back so that others could learn from their mistakes.

Lyndquist knew what was expected—it had been drilled into him—but ignoring these men's screams hadn't been. They were his friends, he was their only chance. The decision was automatic. He quickly lowered the Apollo ship downward toward the submerging vehicle. By the time he arrived the only portion of the ship still visible was the radio antenna, which he quickly latched onto with a mechanical arm. The grip was tenuous, he had to move slowly. Too much thrust would break the antenna, too little might put him in the quagmire alongside them. Carefully firing his lateral rockets, he pulled upward, slowly. Finally the vehicle pulled free, and as he headed for the cooler environment of space, beads of lava dripped from the second ship's hull like drops of brown water.

Once he reached a safe height he tried separating the two ships, but the mechanical arm was welded to the antenna. He wanted to put some distance between them in case there was an explosion, but he was unable to break away. Not only had the two ships become one, but all radio contact was lost and there weren't any signs of life inside. It looked as if they might all be finished.

Minutes passed. He waited, watched. Nothing. His monitors indicated that the ship was rapidly cooling. Once it had reached an acceptable temperature he put on a spacesuit and crossed over. Through the porthole he could see both bodies floating inside. They looked dead, but after cutting the escape hatch away he found they were at least breathing. Neither man responded to stimuli. They were vegetables, physically alive, mentally dead.

Their brains had been cooked by the hyperpyrexia.

The return trip with the living corpses was terrible. Three men's duties were now his. Twenty-hour shifts, four hours sleep, no breaks. He not only had to run the ship, he had to care as best he could for the two crewmen, who mostly sat in a corner and stared out into space. On occasion, he'd have to tie them down or otherwise they'd have spent their vacant hours floating in the cabin wherever the air currents carried them.

In the beginning, he tried speaking to the two men, pretending that they understood ... "What do you think of that? Remember when we used to ...? Why don't you take the next shift?" Nobody talked back. He tried reading to them, hoping to restimulate whatever sparks of brain function might remain, but it was pointless. Finally, frustrated, scared, he began screaming. As loud as he could. He'd kick their lifeless bodies, but nothing he did brought more than an occasional blink or hiccup. As he struggled to survive, they merely breathed the required number of times per minute, ate whenever he took time to feed them and evacuated whenever their bodily functions dictated.

It was a living mausoleum.

Keeping his own sanity, though, wasn't his only problem. Fuel was short. The recovery attempt had left him with critically low levels, and it soon became a daily obsession to calculate the distance to home and strive for better fuel economy. Like a miser, he counted drops of fuel. His best calculations left him a half million miles short of earth's atmosphere, and it appeared he was doomed to a permanent orbit around the sun. He and the two vegetables.

Meanwhile Mission Control had been tracking his progress, and when their computers agreed with his calculations a decision was made to send a shuttle flight out to meet him. The rendezvous had to be at no more than 400,000 miles. Not even a hundred feet more. That would be the maximum distance shuttles could fly out in those days and still make it back home.

The days counted down. Lyndquist shifted to a twenty-four-hour day, rarely took time to eat, constantly monitored the control panel. The slightest deviation from his course could be disastrous. A few solar storms threatened to tip the ship, but each time he managed to compensate. Everything dispensable was jettisoned to limit mass load...he considered eliminating the two crewmen but couldn't make himself do it. In the distance the earth loomed as a distant star. If they were going to make it, they'd do it together.

The shuttle flight reached the rendezvous point first and went into a holding pattern. Inside, a mobile hospital with specialists in hyperpyrexia waited. From Lyndquist's description of his colleagues there was little hope, but the scientists had seen extraordinary recoveries.

At a hundred thousand miles separation, Lyndquist's half million mark, the shuttle ship spotted his lights. At fifty-thousand miles, he was visible on their telescopes but then disappeared at twenty thousand when his engines began to fail. Auxiliary power was all he had left, and at a thousand miles, it too went out. The ship was silent, sliding through frictionless space with oxygen supplies recorded as empty and his cabin temperature rapidly falling. The last thing he remembered before passing out was sealing his spacesuit.

When reached all three men were comatose, and in another few minutes they would have all been dead. The two crewmen did fully recover—thanks to ingenious and persistent efforts. Reprimands were mixed with congratulations. Lyndquist, of course, shouldn't have attempted the rescue, the rules said that he should get a court martial, but that was quickly brushed aside. Instead of stripping him of his rank, they promoted him. The Space Commission badly needed a hero. Lyndquist was made to order....

The intercom was bleeping Lyndquist's name again, and the voice announced that the shuttle flight would be docking in two minutes. Lyndquist glanced into the lower crow's nest, greeted the crewman on duty and hurried back toward the elevator shafts.

VI

October 29, 1991

DR. LEIGH's conversation at his 10 A.M. appointment with the President was brief. The Chief Executive wanted fast answers. Was this serious enough to represent a potential threat to the country's, the world's security, or was it just some quirk, some technological error or misinterpretation that wasn't worth getting excited about? He wanted the investigation kept secret. If the press ever got hold of the story, wild predictions of extraterrestrial visitors were sure to follow.

Within an hour communiques went out to the Mount Wilson Observatory in southern California, the radio antenna tower at Arecibo, Puerto Rico, and the Goddard Space Flight Center at Greenbelt, Maryland. Each group was told to direct its attention to the vicinity of the star Alpha Centauri, to look for anything unusual and to report whatever it found directly to the Commission. Because the investigation was classified, none of the astronomers was told what specifically to look for, only "anything unusual." Even if Dr. Leigh could have been more open, he couldn't have been more specific. At this point, no one knew what to expect.

Meanwhile he also called an emergency meeting of the Commission Board. Six of the ten members were in town and he immediately summoned them. None was told why, just to drop whatever he was doing and come ASAP.

Two hours later the six men were assembled in the conference room. The doors were locked, incoming calls on hold. Included was Dr. Milton Freyberg from the Jet Propulsion Laboratory, Thomas Field from the National Aeronautics and Space Administration, Dr. Eugene Smith from the Kennedy Space Center, General Donald Saunders from the Marshall Space Flight Center and Garibald Fischer, Secretary of Defense.

Dr. Leigh began by showing everyone a copy of the termination signal.

"I think that's great," Dr. Smith said, and then explained. "I mean at least it's still working after all these years and especially all those miles. I'm surprised that it had enough power, but what's this about being entered?"

In answer Dr. Leigh handed out copies of the communications protocol on Pioneer X and directed attention to the last paragraph.

"Harold, this is silly," General Saunders spoke up. "You don't really think someone or something on purpose entered that satellite, do you? It has to be an asteroid collision or something similar."

Mr. Field agreed.

"Look, I don't know what to think," Dr. Leigh told them. "But the President wants an answer." He turned to Dr. Freyberg, who had been part of the original team on the Pioneer series.

Dr. Freyberg uneasily cleared his throat. "I was able to collect most of my notes." He cleared his throat again. "They seem to indicate that the transmitter was installed in a very specific manner. Any random collision would have knocked it out, not set it off. We wanted to know if anyone ever saw the message that it was carrying, a kind of eavesdropping on our part, and we used a trap door mechanism not too different from the one used on the Voyagers. It had to be opened in a very specific, very rational way. Nothing random could do it . . . I think the only possible explanation is that the satellite's had a . . . well, a visitor. . . ."

"Come on, there must be some better answer to this," General Saunders said. "Little Martians still belong in comic strips."

"Maybe, but that satellite's gone way beyond Mars, into an area where we know absolutely nothing about life forms. I suppose it *could* have been a malfunction, I hate to be arbitrary, but there's one thing for sure—"

"What's that," the general pressed.

"If there *was* a . . . visitor, he, it now knows where the

satellite came from, what we look like and how long ago it was launched. If he's at all curious, let's hope he's also friendly."

No one wanted to believe Dr. Freyberg's speculation, but on the other hand it was difficult to counter it. After spending the rest of the day deliberating over all other possibilities, the group finally decided to wait and watch. No one wanted to set off a panic on the basis of mere speculation.

They monitored reports from three government observatories, but after four days nothing unusual had been seen or heard. The silence, possibly a good sign, worried them nonetheless, and on the fifth day the group decided to send a message of their own. A feeler of sorts...

The selected wording was simple. "We come in peace." It was repeated on the hour every hour for twenty-four hours, then stopped while they waited. Two days later, an identical message came in return. "We come in peace." It repeated itself on the hour every hour for twenty-four hours.

To the scientists monitoring the signal, it seemed like an echo, but there had never been an echo from outer space before.

VII

It ALL seemed crazy, Dr. Cortney Miles thought as she stared out through the shuttle ship's porthole. In the distance she could see the revolving Space Lab with its red and blue lights flashing along the rim and panel of lighted cabin windows. Dr. Olmschied had called her two months ago to tell her that he'd given her name to the Space Commission as a research associate, and then a week later called back to tell her that their project had been approved. What project? Why her? He wouldn't say. He claimed time was too short to make an adequate explanation but promised to send the particulars over to her immediately.

That promise had taken four weeks to fulfill, and now, another month later, she was on her way to study reproduction of monkeys in outer space—Jane Goodall in a space suit. Even on earth she was afraid of heights. So far it all seemed like a dream, an absurd dream, and if she hadn't thought so highly of the professor in the first place she probably wouldn't have agreed to come. Now she was stuck, and thinking back on it, probably should have her head examined.

The experimental plan was simple. The protocol called for six Rhesus monkeys to mate under weightless conditions and be followed through their normal gestation period. Afterwards they'd check the offspring for genetic defects. If none, everyone comes home. If more than statistically expected, they stay and find out why. It seemed the professor should easily be able to handle the work alone, but for some unexplained reason he'd insisted she accompany him. He'd even offered to help her the next year when it came time for grant allocations. She appreciated that, but it wasn't really necessary. If he truly needed her, and he assured her that he did, then that in itself was reason enough to go along to help him....

The past few years had seen a considerable change in the twenty-seven-year-old Cortney Miles, a skilled researcher whose long blonde hair and model's figure seemed more suited to a fashion show than a row of test tubes. Her intense blue eyes looked out through glasses that she really didn't need to wear as often as she did. Her skin had a lovely tan. There wasn't a discernible flaw, and if she'd made the slightest effort she could have been stunning. But she didn't. Her life was science, she belonged to an academic nunnery of sorts, though perhaps only partly by choice. Her parents were divorced. Each three times over and there were more steps and halves than she could keep track of. Being the first born, she had witnessed each transition. Hope, love lost, regained, then lost again. It all primed the defense mechanisms to prevent any more hurt. She'd never make the same mistakes they had, she swore to it. And yet there was an inner feeling that she might.

The conflict came out with one Michael Lester, a graduate student she met at a seminar. Before him, dating was only a social event. With him, it was different. He was unassuming, affectionate when she needed it, never pushy. She needed him for all the love she'd missed and he needed her just to be there.

They dated for twelve months, the last six living together. It was a trial period in Cortney's mind. If things didn't work out there'd at least be no court battles or custody hearings. She wasn't about to have a rerun of her youth. She knew that she couldn't take it.

But the relationship worked beautifully. Every day was better than the day before. She opened herself up and found a love inside her that she didn't know existed. The cynicism, the hate...it was all washed away.

The day after Michael proposed the world fell in on her. A laboratory fire put Michael in the hospital with ninety percent burns. For five days she watched him die a slow, painful death. Scarred, mutilated, he left her, also leaving behind the feeling, the conviction that she'd never love a man again. That she never wanted to . . . couldn't afford to.

She sank back into her protective shell and did what she'd always done before when things hurt too much. Find an outlet, throw herself into it totally and forget everything else. By circumstance, that was college. She studied night and day. Having always loved animals, and seeing no possible threat there, she even considered veterinary medicine, but that all changed when she met Dr. Olmschied.

It was during her second year that she heard about a position opening up in Dr. Olmschied's Genetic Laboratory. Being part of the health sciences department herself, the professor's name was unavoidable. In fact, Olmschied was the department. His work was internationally known, and although it was controversial in some places, it was still highly regarded. Much of it also fascinated Cortney. By merely taking a sample of cells from a newborn infant and studying the chromosomal structure within, Olmschied was able to predict the child's ultimate health as an adult.

The clues that led to Olmschied's discovery came from previous transplant work. In order to match up donors and recipients, the compatibility studies had gone beyond mere blood types and down to the DNA strands themselves. At that point it didn't take so much a genius as an astute observer to compile the results and compare them with patient profiles. To everyone's surprise there were some strong correlations, as if life itself was predetermined the moment that the egg and sperm combined.

Rheumatoid arthritis was the first breakthrough. Previously there had been a few rare types of arthritis associated with certain transplant abnormalities, but this was a predictable major illness. Whenever the DLE-27 locus was present in the person's cells, that individual was certain to incur the disease's crippling effects. If subgroup *a* was present, it would occur within the person's first thirty years of life; if subgroup b, it would strike between the ages thirty and fifty; and if subgroup c, sometime after fifty. Once a person's chromosome work was tabulated, predicting his or her future medical history was relatively easy.

It soon became apparent that a similar pattern was true for heart disease. With the DLE-62 locus, a person was likely to have a heart attack before the age of forty. If one smoked or were overweight, didn't exercise or were chronically tense, the process was hurried along. By assessing the different subgroups, Olmschied could predict the heart attack within a three-year period and also offer a good guess at the patient's likelihood of survival. In a sense he'd become a fortune teller, but his crystal ball was well founded in scientific fact. Soon other diseases followed along: emphysema, lung cancer, asthma, kidney stones, cirrhosis, psoriasis, bowel cancer, diverticulosis, pernicious anemia, diabetes, arteriosclerosis, hypertension, hyperthyroidism, goiters, and brain tumors. People didn't much like hearing what he had to tell them. Even the medical community shunned him, claiming that the philosophy of predeterminism was buried with the Marxists, but within a few years most of his predictions came true and people had to take a second look. Not only was the color of a man's hair, his height, his bone structure and parts of his personality inscribed in the genetic codes of DNA within each cell, but his diseases and ultimate death as well. It all was permanently embossed, and to many it was a frightening concept.

Once science accepted the fact that the kinescope into the future was written at the cellular level, his work began to make a major impact on society. Only some of it was good. The prospect of a definite heart attack hanging over a man's life led some to commit suicide. Pills were easier. It was like telling a person that he had an incurable disease and only six months to live. He didn't want the midnight pain and an agonizing death. Likewise, cancer also took its toll in irretrievable depressions long before the actual tumor cells were evident. It was much better to have it come as a surprise than to know that it lingered around the corner. Life-styles also changed dramatically for those with predictable maladies. Knowing that a crippling arthritis was in the cards kept medical students from studying surgery and gifted children from playing the piano. Business executives with the potential for heart disease or ulcers were encouraged to seek other professions and forestall the inevitable. Many men were merely hired or fired according to their genetic makeup. It was too expensive for a large firm to train someone and then lose them, and there was even talk of making genetic screening a requirement much like a curriculum vitae. The more important the job, the less likely that the company would take a chance.

Other changes were more constructive. If the diseases weren't alterable, some preventive steps could be tried to slow the process. For example, potential asthmatics and elderly people with emphysema were told to move to more arid climates. Those with the code for lung cancer had yearly check-ups, which included X-rays and sputum checks, and with early detection, some cures were established. The same was true for breast cancer. A woman with the DLE-37 locus had a fifty percent chance of incurring the tumor by age forty if she breast fed her children, but a ninety percent chance if she didn't and so bottle feeding was on the decline. People with an increased chance for rheumatic fever had frequent throat cultures, whether ill or not. Those with the codes for peptic ulcer disease were advised to avoid alcohol, aspirin, and coffee, and those with possible gallstones were given more appropriate diets.

Olmschied's work also carried over into genetic counseling, where it was probably most valuable. Interested parents were given a genetic identity card much like those of blood donors. Written in graph style was a full profile of their genetic tendencies and when matched up with their spouse's profile, a computer could tell them what the chances were of conceiving an ill-destined child. A less than fifty percent chance for most of the ailments was considered an acceptable risk except in such cases of hemophilia, sickle cell anemia, Tay Sachs, and phenylketonuria. Here, in particular, the government was taking a close look. Too many children were already institutionalized and if they could prevent their births, pain and money could be saved. Genetic counseling was still voluntary, but there was a movement to change that now that proponents were armed with hard facts.

Dr. Olmschied's discoveries had made him a famous man with as many enemies as friends. Those who argued against him pointed out that most of his predictions were only seventy-five percent accurate at best and they didn't want to base their lives on statistics that might not apply to them. Others wanted to redirect their lives to maximize the time that they had. At least this way they had a warning and for that they were thankful. Jobs changed, homes and businesses were sold, money was spent or saved depending on the future prospects and dream vacations embarked on. There wasn't any need to save up for something ten or twenty years down the road when your life expectancy was five years.

To get a position in Olmschied's laboratory, all applicants had to undergo a genetic profile study, but the prospect of knowing the future didn't bother Cortney. In fact, she was curious, but two weeks after a tissue biopsy was taken from the inside of her cheek, she received an urgent notice to see Dr. Olmschied. Reading it, she panicked. None of the other applicants had received a letter and she assumed that its urgency must have meant something bad.

She remembered waiting in his outer office, her nails nearly bitten to their quick. Beyond the glass panelled door she could hear the old man's gruff voice arguing with someone. Both men sounded angry and their shouting made her that much more upset.

After ten minutes the man left in a huff and with some hesitancy she entered in his place. The office was all books, shelves from floor to the ceiling, except a small section for a latticed window and the professor's desk, where he was scrutinizing some term papers. As he noticed her reticent approach, his anger quickly dissipated into a welcoming smile. The change from what she was expecting was dramatic.

"Come in." He motioned her to take a seat across from him. "I hope we didn't alarm you with the letter." He seemed to know who she was without an introduction.

"A little," she nervously confided.

For several seconds the professor merely stared at her, studying each feature, the shape of her head, the texture of her hair. He seemed pleasant enough, but she had the

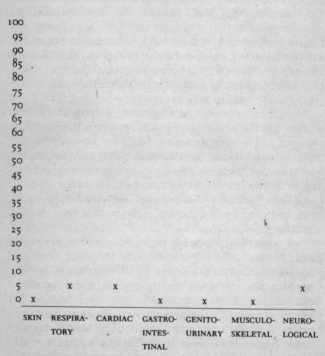

PERCENT CHANCE OF INCURRING DISEASE BY SYSTEM

	SKIN	RESPIRA-TORY	CARDIAC	GASTRO-INTES-TINAL	GENITO-URINARY	MUSCULO-SKELETAL	NEURO-LOGICAL
100							
95							
90							
85							
80							
75							
70							
65							
60							
55							
50							
45							
40							
35							
30							
25							
20							
15							
10							
5		X	X				X
0	X			X	X	X	

feeling that she was some bacterium on the stage of a microscope. His persistence made her feel uneasy, and she kept forcing a smile, waiting for him to speak first.

"Let me assure you that there's no reason for concern," he resumed, seemingly satisfied. "Your profile was perfect, or at least as perfect as a human being can get. It's the best I've seen, and I think if you're not poisoned or run over you should easily make it to ninety. Maybe even a hundred or more."

He pulled a manilla folder from his upper desk drawer, opened it and then showed her a graph. "This is a breakdown of the major diseases by system. Anything under five percent is negligible."

It was a peculiar feeling being told how long she would live, a strange lease on life that was difficult to believe. She was tempted to laugh, to thank him for his palmistry, but she knew how accurate his work had been on others and how seriously he took it. If Dr. Olmschied said that she would live to ninety, she probably would.

"We double-checked the calculations, in case you're worried that we might have made a mistake," Olmschied added, but the thought of an error had never crossed her mind. "That's why I asked you to come here to my office. We need some genetically pure subjects, if you'll pardon the expression. I'm not looking for the perfect Aryan race, only a good laboratory control to compare other subjects with. If you still want that job here, we have room."

Cortney accepted immediately. She definitely needed the position. Not only was it a paying job, but his work was the kind she could lose herself in, dedicate herself to.

Once she started, it didn't take long for her interests to change from veterinary medicine to genetics. There was an enthusiasm in Olmschied's lab that swept her up, probing into the unknown, unraveling it and meeting a challenge from the future. The professor became her personal mentor, and although he was not an outwardly warm person, a genuine affection developed between them. She needed someone, at least a father figure, and he a daughter. Neither would have admitted it, but their mutual feelings were apparent to others who worked around them. The old man seemed to sense her loss, and although it was not his style to verbalize it, his gruffness was a front for the warmth and compassion he managed to communicate quietly to her, and she in turn became increasingly dedicated to him. It was a working relationship that truly worked.

VIII

THE SHUTTLE rocket glided into a landing slot along the outer rim of the Space Lab and immediately joined the rotation scheme. Other than the addition of gravity and a distant clicking sound, the change was barely perceptible. A moment later, the pilot announced that everyone could undo their seat belts and prepare to disembark. Altogether there were fifteen passengers, the ship's maximum.

Cortney was one of the first to stand. Eight straight hours of sitting was more than enough. She quickly stretched and then looked down at Dr. Olmschied, who had been sitting next to her. He was still asleep. His glasses were lying slanted across the bridge of his nose and his head had fallen to one side. After she gave him a nudge he abruptly awoke, promptly straightened his glasses and pretended to have been awake all along.

"It's about time we got there," he muttered, fixing his tie and then automatically checking his right coat pocket. He was looking for his pipe but quickly recalled having left his meerschaum back on earth. Smoking was forbidden on the Lab and it was one of the pleasures that he had to give up to make the trip.

"Home away from home, I guess," Cortney said beneath her breath. The idea of visiting the first experimental station was exciting. As the two exited through the disembarkation corridor, a narrow white tunnel, Commander Lyndquist was waiting at the other end to greet everyone. "Dr. Olmschied?" he asked, recalling the ID pictures that he'd been sent.

"Yes, sir." The old man responded with a glowing smile.

"Welcome to Space Lab," Lyndquist said as he extended his hand to the professor and turned toward Cortney. "And you must be Dr. Miles. Scuttlebutt has it that we'd have a pretty face on board, but I didn't believe it until now. I hope that the flight up wasn't too much for you."

"No, I enjoyed every minute of it," Cortney lied, blocking out the feeling of unease as the shuttle rocket took off and the lingering tension it left in its wake.

"There'll be a brief orientation session in the conference room and then we'll take everyone on a quick tour of the ship," Lyndquist said, and then directed them to one of his crewmen, who would act as their guide. Next he moved to greet Dr. Gregor, who was just disembarking. Walking in line behind the professor, whose dark beard clashed with his naturally blond hair, were two sets of identical twins and a large entourage of research technicians. In fact, most of the passengers on the shuttle flight belonged to Dr. Gregor's team.

"What are the twins for?" Cortney whispered to Olmschied as they both followed the crewman into another corridor that was lined with pictures of the Space Lab in various stages of construction.

"You mean tweedle-dee and tweedle-dum. Conrad's always been known for his bizarre shows. I guess he's going to freeze one of each and keep the other around as a control animal. That way the family won't lose both sons at the same time. He likes to be careful, you know—" Olmschied stopped abruptly, seeming embarrassed by his outburst and yet relieved at having let out some of his disapproving anger.

Cortney was struck by the professor's sarcasm. It was hardly like him to speak so strongly, but for the moment she decided to overlook it. There were too many things to claim her attention . . . This was a wholly new experience, like traveling to a foreign country, and although things were different it wasn't quite the science fiction she expected. The brightly lit corridors reminded her of an airport terminal back home, only here they were considerably cleaner and much quieter. The people were the same, except uniformed. Shades of green were for commissioned ranks, orange and red for crewmen and white for civilians. In addition, each of the crew wore a patch on the left shoulder denoting assignment area: command center, communications, engineering, maintenance, research. Fire doors rose electrically from the floor to the ceiling as they approached and each time they passed through, a woman's simulated voice announced the section they were entering.

The conference room was located the equivalent of a quarter mile from where they disembarked. It was situated along the solar side of the Space Lab, which because it rotated in only one plane had a permanent light side and a permanent dark side. Inside everything was tightly secured to the floor, including the long conference table, the ovoid chairs along both sides and the podium up front. Across from the entry the wall was speckled with tiny portholes that admitted sunlight to illuminate the room.

Cortney and Dr. Olmschied took seats toward the back, and a few minutes later a set of identical redheaded twins sat down across from them. Both smiled as they sat down, giggled in unison and then were identically quiet. The other set, brunettes, sat further up toward the front with Dr. Gregor.

Lyndquist arrived, and after welcoming everyone again and wishing them a productive experience, began the orientation lecture.

"This is Section A. If you look at the handouts on the table in front of you, you can see that the outer rim is divided into four major sections, A, B, C, and D, and each of them is divided into ten smaller sections, each designated with numbers such as A-7. Your living quarters are all located between D-4 and D-10, which is a long way around if you turn left outside these doors, but less than a city block's walk if you go right. You'll learn the shortest routes with time and practice but in the meantime if you start off wrong it's only a mile and a half around. Our command post, Communications, and the center for astronomical studies is in Section B. The ship's infirmary is in C, headed by Dr. McLaughlin, and most of the crew's quarters are located in Section D.

"The ship has a built-in communications system with video receivers every fifty yards in the main corridor and in every room as well. Calls to the earth, however, will have to be cleared through the command post. There are only a few hours each day that the frequencies are open. Mail will be forwarded to the computers in your rooms, directly from earth. It's more efficient than the old postman, and you can be assured that everything you receive is confidential.

"Also, you'll note on your diagrams that the emergency cubicles are located near most of the video receivers. The entry doors are painted a bright red so that you can't miss them. In case of an accident where oxygen levels are affected or pressure is lost, an alarm will sound and you should immediately head for the nearest cubicle. There will be an unannounced drill while you're here. Each of these cubicles has been equipped with enough supplies to sustain thirty people a minimum of five days. That's the average number of people expected to enter each one, but needless to say, some cubicles may end up with more and others with fewer. We estimate that it would take a week for the shuttle flights to evacuate everyone. I'm sure you don't have to worry, though."

Cortney half-smiled toward the professor. "I sure hope so."

Lyndquist continued on to discuss the gravity scheme on the ship, the cafeteria-style eating with limited menus and lastly the small living quarters, "well-equipped but more for sleeping than living in."

After opening the floor to questions for a few minutes, he took the group on a tour beginning in Hydroponics, an auditorium-sized room that was solid fern plants.

"This is where we get our oxygen supply," the commander said once everyone had caught up. "They're good exchangers of carbon dioxide for oxygen. Also their spores germinate easily so the crop is constantly maintained. We grow them with the nutrient film technique, a process developed in the Sahara Desert about seven years ago for use on barren land. There are several steps that our water passes through before nurturing these plants. First, all used water from the ship is sterilized by sunlight in special reservoirs along the periphery of the ship. This takes about a day. Then while it's still warm it's cycled through the ship to heat the interior. From there it's fed down here into narrow troughs. If you'll look closely you'll see that none of the plants is rooted in soil."

Cortney bent down to look into one of the Plexiglas troughs. As far as she could see there were dangling roots seated in less than an inch of trinkling water.

"The process works better than dirt. The nutrients are there, mostly from our wastes, without the extra problem of handling or even carrying the soil up from earth. Not only does it work better than dirt but all of our plants are free of disease. Occasionally we add whatever nutrients our chemists tell us are missing but usually the recycled water is enough. There are about three ferns for every person on board. Our oxygen percent is twenty-three or two points above what you're used to. It gives us an edge in case of trouble and I'm sure you won't notice the difference."

The next stop was the vegetable gardens, where the same nutrient film technique was utilized. Lettuce, tomatoes, carrots, peas, spinach, potatoes, beans, beets, corn, and wheat were all found in separate rooms, each set at different temperatures and each exposed to varying periods of sunlight through retractable overhead shades. "They're no seasons up here. We harvest the corn twice yearly, wheat three times, and most of the vegetables year round. Whenever we stick a seed in the film, we get a plant. Here we manipulate nature, not the reverse."

After going another hundred yards, they came to several gigantic aquariums stocked with millions of tiny shrimp. "These are our filters," Lyndquist said. "Fifty tons of living, breathing filters that clean our water. They'll scavenge anything and reproduce so quickly that they've also become our main staple of food. Fried, boiled, baked, broiled, flambé. Anyway you can think of, our chefs will accommodate. You may find it a little tiresome though."

Everyone laughed appropriately except Dr. Olmschied, who hated shrimp. In fact he disliked all shell fish and muttered his annoyance as the group continued along the circular path to the guts of the ship—the solar-driven turbines.

"These babies are our energy source or at least where the sun's energy is converted into usable electricity. We get about a quad of electrical energy a year or the equivalent of a hundred and fifty million barrels of oil. Some of the water that comes through the aquariums is used to cool the turbines. The rest goes to the ship for general use and then back again through the cycle. Except for spare parts, we're practically self-sustaining."

The rest of the tour included maintenance and storage, neither of which was unusual other than that they occupied half of the inner space. Seeing that the group was tiring, the commander suggested that they stop. No one argued. It had been a long day.

Cortney, in particular, was looking forward to a rest. The previous night's apprehension had kept her awake. She looked forward to a hot bath and a good bed. Enticing thoughts. Neither was in her future.

As she entered her assigned room she was stunned—despite Lyndquist's warning—by its small size and emptiness. Other than her two bags of luggage on the floor, the room was bare. The walls were metal, smooth and dull gray, with a collage of different-shaped handles as if she'd stepped into a room whose walls were solid with cabinets. Above, the ceiling was luminescent and below, a dark green Velcro. The room was a metal box with lights and cushioning. Even the porthole was tiny, and judging by the darkness beyond, she knew that she was situated on the dark side of the satellite. Although she had never suffered from claustrophobia before, she now felt trapped.

Included in the handout that Lyndquist had given

them was a diagrammatical representation of each room's layout. Supposedly they were all identical and equipped with everything they needed, but it seemed just too small, too confining, too *empty*.

The sleeping cot was a longitudinal shelf that folded up against the wall beneath the porthole. After unlatching the metal hooks, she lowered the two-meter slab down to the horizontal where it automatically locked into place. On top was a thin mattress completely enveloped in a burgundy blanket, sleeping bag style, and across them both were two leather straps. It looked like a straitjacket. But it really wasn't the security measures or the bed's austerity that bothered her so much. The slab took up half her room. When down, there was even less space to move about in.

After returning the cot to its closed position she began to investigate the walls. Pulling on one of the larger handles, she found another folding shelf, which turned out to be a desk with a free-swinging stool beneath. Across its top were dozens of Velcro straps and a stenciled note reminding her to be sure that everything she used was always kept secured. Further along, she found several closed shelves with plastic grips for holding books, a large viewing screen for communication and entertainment, a computer terminal with dual options for the Space Lab's system or Mission Control at Houston, and a music storage bank whose memory crystals housed recordings as far back as the 1920's. Whatever her mood, she merely made a selection on the typewriter and the computer took care of the rest. If she didn't know, she could merely give the computer her mood, and it would make the selections. Along the opposite wall she found storage closets for her personal belongings and a set of white uniforms wrapped in cellophane. Above was a shelf marked for toiletries with another warning: nothing scented or powdered was to be used. She assumed that they were worried about the ventilation system.

Maybe, she thought, it was just fatigue at the bottom of all this . . . usually she wasn't so irritable. She wandered over to the porthole and looked out. Far beneath was the earth, about the size of a child's beachball, beautifully blue and wrapped in wisps of cotton. She knew that she should be excited, enthralled, overwhelmed. Instead she was . . . sad. And worried. And she didn't have an inkling why.

IX

A SECOND radio communique was sent from Cyclops, a newly built circular mass of 900 separate radiotelescopes that were expressly designed for future interstellar communications. This time, however, the wording was changed. Instead of saying "We come in peace," they radioed "We live in peace." With it they hoped to clarify the previous confusion. No one knew if the returned signal meant that somewhere...something was also coming in peace, if there was any "someone" or "something," or if it really was just an echo as it sounded.

As before, two days elapsed and then came the response. "We live in peace." Again it was an exact duplication, another echo, without explanation. For an unknown reason their radio beams seemed to be striking a distant mirror an estimated sixteen billion miles away that was previously thought to be empty space. Not only was it beyond the outer limits of earth's solar system, but it was also billions of miles short of the nearest star. Nothing was known to be there—at least nothing that one could either see or measure.

Still, most of the Board members began to relax. Two duplications in both wording and timing had to be an echo and not another intelligent life's way of communication. They suggested that it might be a stellar storm or comet's tail, something that could destroy the satellite and set up enough of a disturbance to reflect radio beams. Dr. Freyberg disagreed, and when Dr. Leigh argued in support, he was accused of invoking H. G. Wells. The idea that some alien race in furthest space had taken a screwdriver and wrench to the Pioneer was laughable, but to appease Freyberg and Leigh the others agreed to set up two monitoring stations in the Northern and Southern Hemispheres. Just in case.

X

JOHN HICKS awoke several minutes ahead of his alarm but his excitement had kept him tossing most of the night and it was only during the last hour that he had fallen asleep. As he lifted his shade to light the room, a beam of sunlight shot through the circular opening and bounced off his walls. The glare was almost too bright to tolerate, but he loved it. After overcoming Dr. Baumeister's surprise two months before, he'd been counting the days until takeoff. This was going to be a tremendous adventure. Coming up on the shuttle flight, he felt like a little boy again sneaking around the presents on the night before Christmas. He just couldn't wait.

As far back as he could recall, he'd been fascinated with space exploration. He'd seen every movie, studied documentaries and read every book he could get his hands on. When he was seven he wanted to be an astronaut. For years he followed the long succession of Apollo flights, the Viking probes, Mariner explorations and the advent of the Sky Labs. When he was twelve he even tried building his own rocket, a baton and some gun powder, but a two-foot hole blasted through the garage door dampened those efforts. As he grew older, childhood notions were pushed aside by practicalities. They were never forgotten, though, only pushed aside....

Now, after putting on robe and slippers, he headed for the showers. It was five minutes past six on his watch, 0605 space time. Breakfast was scheduled for 0700, but he wanted some time beforehand to look around. Having been on the second shuttle flight to arrive the previous night, his orientation session was brief and so far he hadn't seen much more than a few corridors and his own room. Commander Lyndquist had asked that no one wander around until he'd met with them again.

When Hicks arrived at the washroom he found Dr.

Baumeister already in the shower. The older surgeon greeted him exuberantly, adding, "The soap's a little scratchy but the water's nice and warm."

"It's probably biodegradable." Hicks answered as he began looking around for a stall.

"There aren't any," Baumeister told him, "you've got to sit down." He seemed vastly amused.

Ensconced in one of the cubicles, Hicks noted a sign warning about the suction. Simultaneously, the pressure on the toilet seat triggered a loud vacuum that nearly sucked him into the bowl. This monstrous coprophagic machine was literally pulling his innards out of him.

Shaking his head in disbelief afterwards, he crossed to the sink, washed his hands and tried the Lab's version of toothpaste. It looked like raspberry, but after brushing it around for a minute, it had a distinctly fishy flavor.

"Ready to start working?" Baumeister asked as Hicks stepped into the next shower stall and began to dry off.

"If the morning ablutions don't kill me first."

The shower water came out in timed spurts, amounts calculated to soak and then after sudsing, a similar blast to rinse off. A gallon per man per shower.

"A few days of that acclimitization training and then off to the O.R. The dogs ought to arrive sometime later today," Baumeister said.

"Dogs and monkeys both, I hear."

"The monkeys are Olmschied's. The old man's studying the effects of outer space on reproduction. It might be interesting to keep tabs on their work."

"It might also be a good idea to keep a safe distance in case he comes up with any monsters."

Fifteen minutes later Hicks was back in his room putting on the Space Lab uniform. It was comfortable, very lightweight and smooth to the touch, but strange too.

As he exited his room and started toward the observation deck he caught a glimpse of Cortney Miles en route to the women's showers. From the distance, he could barely make out her features, but the figure beneath her tight robe and long blonde hair was clear enough.

Whoever she was, he knew he wanted to meet her. Before coming to the Space Lab he'd resigned himself to at least a temporary celibacy, but now with images of what he thought he saw, there was a glimmer of hope for a change in plans.

The observation deck was located just above the command post and it extended the full width of the outer rim. At each end was a huge viewing window and in between, lounging chairs—a sort of mini-theater from which to watch the celestial show with pictured programs placed next to each chair to explain the passing scene.

As Hicks entered the room, he was stunned by the sight. To his right was the earth and to his left, the glowing fires of the sun. He very much felt as though he could reach out and touch them both. He just stood there in amazement, frozen in his steps, and waited until both bodies had rotated downward and were replaced by a blanket of glittering stars. Millions of lights. More than he'd ever seen before on a clear night on earth. Before him Sirius glowed like a fifty-carat diamond set on a black velvet pad, Hercules was obviously muscle-bound and Taurus on the run. Every constellation that he could identify was just beyond the porthole. Every planet. Whatever he missed on the first revolution, he caught on the second and third. It was like a giant kaleidoscope, each view more exciting than the one before it. Each one more hypnotizing.

He stayed until the chimes for breakfast sounded, but promised himself that he'd come back later.

When he arrived in the dining room, the food was already laid out across the serving table buffet style. Scrambled eggs, link sausage, selections of juice, and buttered toast. As he helped himself to sizeable portions of each, he asked a nearby waiter if the eggs were real. Amused with the question, the man shook his head and explained that everything was a derivative of vegetables.

Dr. Baumeister arrived a few minutes later, hurried through the line and sat next to him. He sounded disappointed. "I tried to get permission to see the amphitheater ahead of time but they won't let any of us out there yet." He was his usual impatient self. He knew they had to undergo the five days of acclimitization, but felt that *he* didn't need it.

As they began eating, Cortney entered. Even though she was obscured by others, Hicks immediately recognized her. He'd been watching for that blonde hair; she was even lovelier than he'd hoped.

"You know who that is?" he asked Baumeister, pointing his fork in her direction.

Baumeister shrugged his shoulders, smiling as he turned to study her profile.

Hicks watched as she slowly passed through the line, hoping to ask her to join them, but Dr. Olmschied came in just as she finished and called out to her instead. She waited at the front of the line and then the two of them moved to a distant table.

"They'll be plenty of time," Baumeister said, noticing his colleague's interest and recognizing the professor. "That's Dr. Olmschied. You'll have plenty of time. And opportunity."

XI

AFTER BREAKFAST they were divided into two groups—
John's for an orientation tour, Cortney's to begin the
acclimitization program.

"The first stage today will be at eighty percent normal
gravity," Lyndquist said once the second group had
assembled outside the West elevator. "We'll be going to
the fourth level inward. It's not much of a change but you
should feel a little lighter. You'll be able to jump a little
higher and walk further distances without tiring. At this
level free floating will be impossible, but I want everyone
to wear the Velcro shoes anyway. You'll have to get used
to them for the next stages."

After the plastic packets with sandals were handed out
and everyone had them securely fastened around their
shoes, Lyndquist allowed six people into the elevator at a
time. It was slow going and when it came time for the last
six, Cortney and Drs. Gregor and Olmschied were among
them. The two scientists were barely cordial to each other.

When the elevator stopped at the fourth level Cortney
could feel the reduced hold of gravity. When she stood,
there was more spring in her legs, and an unusual feeling
of buoyancy to her body. Eager to try it out, she jumped
from the elevator door and found herself gliding to a spot
seven feet away.

Olmschied too could feel the buoyancy and there was a
distinct smile of pleasure on his face. The pain in his right
knee was gone and with it, the need to limp. The decreased
weight on the ailing joint was like a shot of novocaine. He
could actually walk like a normal person again. Even if
the trip proved not to have been necessary, this alone
would have made it worthwhile.

Waiting for them was a three-hundred-meter obstacle
course rigged with up and down stairs of variable width
and different slants, pitch-dark rooms with traps, tunnels,

some of which were revolving, and a sundry of barriers concocted to test even the most athletic men on earth. Here they were easier, and as Cortney handled the challenge with relative ease, she was surprised to see that the professor was not far behind her. Only one tunnel tripped him up, but only momentarily as he quickly righted himself and resumed the pace as if nothing had happened.

A lecture on adjusting to problems of weightlessness was given by the ship's physician, Dr. McLaughlin, a short, heavyset ex-general practitioner with a peppery gray beard and a salty manner. Listening to him speak, Cortney decided she liked him. He was sort of a throwback to an old sea captain haranguing the recruits as he went through his repertoire of fist-pounding, flailing gestures, spirited pacing back and forth.

In substance he warned against leaving equipment unsecured, liquids uncovered and powders open. He also didn't want anyone flying through the air unless they had God-given wings and he didn't want anyone hurrying unless someone's life was at stake. Everything was a no-no. To maintain a safe environment under weightless conditions, everything had to be done slowly and carefully. Too many people had already been hurt learning that basic lesson.

On the way back through the same obstacle course Cortney found herself walking next to the redheaded twins, Dennis and Donald Simpson. Curious about Dr. Gregor's work, she began asking questions about the Stanford professor's work, but the twins' answers were at best sketchy. They knew that one of them would be put in suspended animation for a month's time, but didn't know or care which one it would be. Each would accept whichever role was delegated to him. When asked why, they merely said that either assignment would be fun. It struck her odd that they'd be so willing, so tranquil, almost as if they'd been drugged, but they seemed to know what they were doing and otherwise seemed like pleasant, normal teenagers.

Once everyone was reassembled at the elevator doors they were directed to a makeshift tool shop where a series of demonstrations were set up to emphasize the real dangers in ordinary activity. The first example was hammering. Under normal gravity conditions a hammer would hit a nail and stay there unless purposefully lifted away by its user. In outer space the rebound phenomenon sent the tool flying back toward the user. With a saw, the carrythrough inertia was even more striking and if not properly controlled could easily go on to sever a leg. The same was true for most of the cutting utensils that required a little pressure to work; the trick was always to use a safe backing to resist the blade's forward progress.

At 1200, day one of the acclimitization for Cortney's group ended. The second group would take the afternoon session and tomorrow they'd move on to the sixty percent level.

As Cortney waited to exit the elevator at the outer rim, her feet felt heavy. They seemed to be weighted down, and as she stepped out she felt clumsy. They'd move the way they should, only she had to think about it and make a special effort, and when she got back to her room she quickly flipped her shoes off to compensate. Beneath, she could see that her feet were pale, turning pink as blood was just beginning to return to them. The pins and needles feeling was almost unbearable.

In the back of her mind, though, she was still intrigued by Gregor's experiment. At least curious. She wanted to know more, and recalling Dr. Olmschied's sarcasm, she doubted that he'd be much help to her. She turned to the computer and typed in Gregor's name and cross-referenced it with a history of his present work. A minute later she had two typewritten sheets of notes. She tucked her feet in under her on the cot and began to read.

Conrad Gregor, M.D., Ph.D.
Medical Degree: Columbia, 1978
Doctor of Philosophy: M.I.T., 1981

Primary work: Cryosuspension
Background:

Hypothermia antedates history, but the first recording of its use was by Aulius Cornelius around 180 AD At the time, people suffering from serious maladies with elevated skin temperatures were dunked into vats of freezing water. The heated body was obviously the cause for their other problems and by cooling it, everything would return to normal. The cure killed most of the victims, but there were a few survivors and they seemed to give credence to his thesis.

Another example occurred during the Third Crusade when Richard the Lion-Hearted succumbed to desert fever. Although Sultan Saladin was his archenemy, upon hearing of the warrior's ailment, procured a dozen camels and carried snow down from the mountain tops to aid him. His entrance into Richard's encampment was a surprise, but they'd heard about cooling and allowed the Sultan's physicians to try it. Days later he recovered, and now in retrospect we assume that it probably was heat prostration which even today is treated with cooling.

Later, Dr. Currie and others used cooling for the treatment of a variety of tropical fevers and actually enjoyed a moderate amount of success. During the 1950's, the French used a similar method to transport their seriously wounded from the battlefields in Indochina to distant and much better equipped hospitals behind the lines. On arrival the soldiers were immediately rewarmed and treated. The survial statistics were markedly improved, and it was assumed that the cooling had slowed the body's metabolism in such a way that the effect of blood loss had been diminished.

During the 1960's and into the 1970's, transplant operations took advantage of the cooling techniques. Kidneys from donors were shown to survive in excess of two hours if cooled between 77 and 68 degrees Fahrenheit. Later, during heart transplant procedures, it was shown that the entire body can be cooled for prolonged periods without ill effects. The Darnall heart transfer to Washkansky in Cape Town, South Africa, is a typical example. The donor's heart was ultimately cooled to 50 degrees and the recipient later survived for thirteen days, dying of pneumonia and not a cardiac problem. Subsequent heart transplants lived as long as eight and nine years.

In the same manner, the brain can also be frozen. At normal temperatures it can only survive for four minutes without oxygen, but at 86 degrees it will easily last eight to ten minutes; at 80 degrees a full ninety minutes, and at 50 degrees it will endure two to three days. Recent therapy toward serious brain damage has been seen in cases where the older therapy was certain to fail. This is also true of disease of the central nervous system, such as multiple sclerosis, cerebral palsy, amyotrophic lateral sclerosis, and spinal cord injuries. If treated early enough, most victims will regain full use of their paralyzed limbs and all pain is gone.

During the early 1980's, Dr. Gregor's work included the use of hypothermia in the therapy of cancer. It was known that tumors required higher amounts of oxygen and nutrients than the victim's body and thereby the tumor was easily destroyed. Only leukemias are resistant, such as the Karen Olmschied case where the girl died during the freezing procedure.

Before Gregor's work, the lowest temperature recorded was 48.2 degrees and the level was maintained for forty-five minutes. Using tetrahydroepandroic chloride (THEC), however, he was able to lower body temperatures to 33 degrees, one degree above freezing, and to keep them there for as long as ten years. His work had now progressed into suspended animation for the terminally ill, and thus far he owns and runs seventeen human banks across the country. His depositors total 5000, with additional cases being added each day to his waiting list. Ninety-eight cases have been retrieved and all but one was cured of illness. That patient was refrozen until a later date.

Present Work:

Dr. Gregor's work has shifted to intergalactic survival, and he is scheduled to do experiments on Space Lab V with two sets of identical twins. His preliminary calculations show that an astronaut traveling through space must breathe 1.13 pounds of oxygen each day, drink two liters of water and eat 1.14 pounds of dehydrated or freeze-dried food. With cryosuspension, or artificial hibernation, the oxygen needs fall to 0.04 pounds a day and the needs for food and water are virtually eliminated. In addition, according to Dr. Gregor, the mental stress of daily boredom will not take its toll. The astronaut will merely be awakened on arrival at his destination by a watchful computer, be as healthy as when he took off and not be a day older. He expects to demonstrate this to the Space Commission on a miniaturized scale.

It wasn't all the answers, but it certainly gave her some insight. Looking back to the Olmschied reference, she reread the sentence and then punched the girl's name into the computer. Much to her shock, the girl turned out to be the professor's daughter—died at age nineteen of leukemia during an experiment in cryotherapy. The signature on the death certificate was Conrad Gregor's.

XII

November 11, 1991

GENERAL BOELLING, returning from lunch, received an
urgent call from one of the consoles in Satellite
Monitoring. Radio contact was reported lost with
Voyager I. His presence in the control room was
requested immediately. The ship was a more sophisticated version of the Pioneer X model, it traveled a similar
trajectory past Jupiter and Saturn, and in addition to
carrying a plaque, it also contained a sound-and-light
show with a variety of images and tracings taken from life
on earth: pictures of human anatomy, descriptions of
human conception, mathematical formulae, a picture of
the Snake River in Idaho, the sounds of a busy street, a
whale's cry, the cries of a newborn baby, a string quartet
playing Beethoven, and a greeting from the Secretary
General of the United Nations and the President of the
United States. Everything an extra-terrestial would want
to know.

As Boelling changed directions and descended the
nearest stairwell, he recalled the last time they'd had
trouble—about three months ago as the satellite was
passing through the heliosphere, the transition point
between the end of the sun's gravitational effect and the
beginning of interstellar space; suddenly the camera had
gone dead. For years it had been sending back pictures of
planets and moons never seen before, then one day,
nothing. No fadeout, no blurring, no warning. Radio
contact continued, however, and otherwise suggested that
the satellite was still in good working order.

Now, he discovered, that was gone. The monitor was
working. The satellite had died. Of course, they all did
eventually. Not even a eulogy was in order, only more
paperwork and a cellulose coffin in Archives.

That insouciant attitude persisted for only one day. Precisely twenty-four hours later, Mission Control received another radio signal: "This is a present from a small, distant world, a token of our sounds, our science, our images, our music, our thoughts, and our feelings. We are attempting to survive our time so that we may live into yours. We hope someday, having solved the problems we face, to join a community of galactic civilizations. The record represents our hope and our determination."

The voice was the President's, his recording on Voyager I, and it echoed every hour for another twenty-four until it died and the airwaves were quiet again.

XIII

A FEW minutes before the dinner bells chimed, the shuttle flight carrying the laboratory animals arrived. Inside were twelve Dalmatians and six Rhesus monkeys, and traveling with them was a Filipino caretaker by the name of Nester San Quesito, a short, dark-complected man. He had already gone through the acclimitization program a month before, then returned to earth to collect the animals. Because none of them had experienced weightlessness before, he was expecting the worst.

Several precautionary measures had been taken. The first was sandpapering the animals' calloused paws so they'd automatically stick to the Velcro padding that lined their cages and thereby do away with the need for sandals, which they were certain to tear off. Their cages had been made small to minimize free floating, and all of them had been taught to drink water from plastic bottles. On earth, such training and methods worked beautifully, once in outer space, all hell broke loose.

After overcoming the initial G forces of takeoff, the loss of gravity immediately put the animals into free suspension. Some of the dogs managed to stick with one or two paws, leaving them standing on a slant, while others left the bottoms of their cages entirely and could be seen floating sideways or upside down. The same was true of the monkeys, although most of them were able to grab onto the sides of their cases for some stability. Animal screams filled the ship's interior, excrement came floating through the air. Nester tried to calm the frightened animals and vacuum the cluttered air at the same time. It was a losing battle.

When they finally reached the Space Lab and gravity returned, the animals calmed some. Nester knew their silence was only temporary as he started unloading. All eighteen cages were shifted on to a rolling cart and then wheeled to the South elevator. Once inside Nester began bracing himself for another onslaught. First the doors closed and the animals became quiet. As it started up, the complaints increased, and once they stopped and weightlessness was on them, the cramped quarters became a bedlam of howls and screeches.

Fortunately two crewmen were waiting to help him unload at the other end, and within five minutes all the animals were secured in their new home, a common room between Dr. Baumeister's and Dr. Olmschied's laboratories. Each cage was attached to a special suctioning vent to catch loose debris and each animal was given a new supply of food.

Back along the outer rim, Cortney was in her room debating what to wear to the Captain's dinner. Everyone she'd spoken to was going in uniform, including Dr. Olmschied, who'd been making disparaging remarks about the "nylon pajamas" all day. If he wasn't going to change, she thought, then she might as well not either.

After putting her hair up and changing her glasses for contacts, she locked her door and headed for the dining room. On the way she heard a familiar voice. "Very chic." She turned to see Dr. McLaughlin, dressed up in a tuxedo as if he were on his way to the Met.

"Oh, I knew I should have changed—"

The ship's doctor assured her he just liked to take every excuse to dress up, that it made him feel like he was on a holiday. Unconvinced, Cortney insisted on returning to her room, where she quickly changed into a pink chiffon dress.

In the dining room, she realized Dr. McLaughlin was right. Everyone but he was still wearing their uniforms. Too late to retreat. She hesitated in the doorway as he came over from across the room.

"From chic to ravishing," McLaughlin said, holding up his glass in toast. "Can I get you a drink? If we don't have it, I'm sure we can fake it. The bartender's an expert in potable forgeries."

"I'll have one of yours," she said, but doubting that she was the straight bourbon type, he fetched her a whisky sour, then proceeded to take her around and introduce her to everyone whose name he could remember. Those he didn't, he merely pulled his bifocals out from beneath his coat and read the embossments on their uniforms.

Among the introductions were members of the Banholzer team, who were there to study Bok globules, and the Burget team, on hand to measure waves in the solar winds. When they reached Drs. Baumeister and Hicks, Hicks had his back to her, a ploy when he'd seen her coming. But as he turned, his elbow accidentally knocked the whisky sour into her dress.

After stammered—and genuine—apologies, Hicks hurried to the nearest table, dunked a cloth napkin in the water glass but Cortney wouldn't have anything to do with his repairs . . . or him. She hated the smell of alcohol on her dress, not to mention the icy feeling oozing through her bra and trickling down her skin underneath. When Hicks made a gesture to wipe the spill from her, she backed away and crashed into a table. Everyone in the room had stopped to watch, Cortney could feel their eyes trained on her. She thought she'd scream if Hicks came near her one more time. She had to get out of there, but as she started toward the door Commander Lyndquist went to the front of the room and announced that dinner was being served. She was trapped.

Fortunately Professor Olmschied was standing a few feet away, and she immediately latched onto his arm, using it in part as a shield to cover the wet dress. He looked at her, surprised, she smiled back nonchalantly, and he went on with his conversation with a neuropsychiatrist from U.C.L.A. ". . . what if one of them tried to jump out?"

"Then it's too late."

"Then shouldn't you be doing something sooner?" Cortney broke in, not at all sure what they were talking about, but determined to be part of their discussion and *out* of the spotlight.

"Yes, of course," the other man said, and Dr. Olmschied decided to introduce her. He had no choice as she was practically on top of both of them. The neuropsychiatrist's name was Dr. Stull, and he was there to study the effects of astrophobia.

"A fear of stars?" Cortney asked the wiry professor, whose thick glasses distorted the face behind.

"Literally, perhaps, but actually it's an overwhelming urge to jump out into space," Stull explained as the three moved the nearest chairs and sat down. "To make an analogy, it's the same feeling that people get when they look down from the top of a skyscraper. An urge to jump off."

"Or like an ocean liner?" Cortney added.

"Exactly, except in a satellite in space other lives can be endangered. If a man jumps from a building, an unfortunate pedestrian or two might be hit, but up here the pressure changes and oxygen losses could kill hundreds and probably suck half the equipment out into space."

"Paul's here at the request of the Space Commission," Olmschied explained. "There have been two attempts in the past and they've sent him up here to figure out some way to either prevent any new ones or at least sort out the vulnerable crew members and send them back to earth."

"Correct," Stull said. He enunciated every syllable precisely.

"And why didn't they tell us about this lover's leap ahead of time?" Cortney asked, spotting Hicks sitting down across from her.

"They didn't want to scare anyone off," Stull said, risking a slight grin. "I suspect that anyone tempted would already have tried...except perhaps the new group, the researchers...well, if it's any consolation, no one's succeeded yet. This ship is pretty secure. We may have to worry about someone going stir crazy, but I doubt that anyone will successfully jump."

Both Hicks and Baumeister were now sitting across from her in full view.

"Are you okay? I'm really sorry," Hicks whispered across the table in apparent sincerity. "I'd offer to buy you a new one, but I don't think there's a shopping center too close by."

Cortney smiled, not meaning to.

"You're studying genetics?"

"Yes." Her answer was purposefully curt.

"In monkeys, right?"

"Yes."

"Why not just go to humans?" Baumeister interrupted, eavesdropping, and directing his question to Olmschied. "That's where your work's ultimately headed, isn't it."

"Humans are the last experiment, not the first," the professor told him. "Too much is still unknown and as long as we have time on our side, I don't see any reason to be hasty."

"Sooner or later, you'll have to do the studies on humans, no matter what results you get."

"That's too broad . . . 'no matter what results we get.' No, there are several eventualities that would stop me."

Baumeister could tell by the professor's tone that he shouldn't push the subject, but he personally did feel that they were wasting their time with monkeys. If he were in charge of the investigation, he'd have skipped the hairy facsimiles.

As the conversation shifted to more mundane topics and people spoke about their lives back on earth, Cortney remained quiet. Intermittently, Hicks tried to spark some reaction from her, but the harder he tried, the more she resisted. If she were trying to make him feel guilty rotten, she had succeeded, but if she were trying to discourage him, she had failed. He only wanted to know her better.

XIV

THE REMAINING four days of acclimitization went by quickly for Cortney and by the last stage, zero gravity, she was grateful that the Space Commission had required the gradual adjustment. To have gone straight into the laboratory and been forced to learn everything there by trial and error would have been disastrous. This way, she felt comfortable making the transition.

The training period had also given her a chance to meet most of the researchers, who in general were an overwhelmingly enthusiastic group. To them, this was the beginning of a new scientific era, a Columbian voyage to another New World, and it was hard not getting caught up in their excitement. Certain of them stood out more than others, such as Dr. Gregor, although in his case in a negative way. He was obsessed, rarely staying for the after-dinner chats and whenever he graced them with his time, it was usually to offer a complaint. Everything or anything could be wrong from noisy crewmen or faulty equipment to the wrong type of cheese in his sandwich. Everything seemed to displease him, and it soon became obvious to everyone on board that it was best just to avoid him.

By contrast, the Simpson twins were most affable, rough-and-tumble types who reminded her of her two brothers back home. Somehow they seemed out of place, belonging more on a basketball court or under the fender of an old jalopy, not experimenting with their lives. They really didn't know much about what they were getting into. If it were she, she'd know every detail and then some, but their attitude was lackadaisical. She'd noted it before with curiosity. Now it bothered her, and she decided to try to get to the bottom of it.

But every time she got the boys alone, Gregor came by and took them away. He seemed to always know where they were, what they were doing and whom they were speaking to. Certain people were clearly taboo, and she seemed to be one of them. At dinner they sat at a separate table and immediately afterward went off to bed. Ostensibly it was to keep them in top physical shape, but Cortney had her doubts. He had to be hiding something.

Her answer came on the fifth night, the evening before they moved into the laboratories. A nervous stomach had led her to look for some bicarb of soda from the kitchen. When she got there the lights were out and she had trouble finding the switch. As she moved her fingers along the wall, a crashing sound inside stunned her. Her impulse was to run, but her fingers persisted until she found the switch, and lying on the floor in front of her was one of the Simpson boys—Dennis, she guessed—with an overturned stool next to him.

"Whew," he said, standing up and righting the chair. "For a moment there I thought it was..."

"Gregor?" Cortney finished the sentence. The relief was apparent on both of their faces.

"Yeah. I don't think he'd be too happy if he found me here with these." The boy showed her a handful of cookies he'd foraged from the pantry. "I was just climbing down when you came in. Half scared me to death. I thought for sure it was him. You won't tell him, will you?"

"No, but why's he so strict with you?"

The boy shrugged. "I don't know, he says it's for our own good. Do you believe, he even checks to see if we're asleep at night. I came down here right after he left. I don't know what he'd do if he knew I snuck out. You won't tell him?"

"Mum's the word, but there is one thing you can do for me. I can't figure out why you and your brother are even here. I know my brothers wouldn't be within ten miles of Gregor and his rules."

The boy seemed uneasy. "That's something I'm not supposed to tell anyone."

"Some type of government secret, I suppose." Cortney tried to play it light, but Simpson didn't laugh.

"No."

"Then money? He's offered you a fortune."

"Not really." The boy hesitated, as if to consider how much he could trust her. Finally he said, "It's because of mom. If I tell you, you've got to promise not to tell anyone else."

Cortney nodded.

"Mom's dying. At least she was until Dr. Gregor found us. It's some type of cancer that's spread through her whole body. The doctors said she only had a few more weeks to live, but now she's got a chance. Dr. Gregor found out about us and called dad one night. The next day, he put her into suspension for free."

"You mean in a *trade* for you and your brother's help on this experiment?"

"It's the only chance that she has. We'd do it a dozen times. He's a little hard to understand, his rules and all, but without him, our mother would never have had a chance."

"And the other boys. Somebody sick in their family too?"

"Their sister. They're triplets really. I'm not sure what she's got, but it's affecting her brain and she's losing her eyesight. Gregor got her into suspension just in time."

"Just in time for his experiment, you mean." But the boy was already hurrying back to his room. Well, at least now it was clear why he was keeping them away from everyone. If anything happened to those boys, she promised herself to see to it that Gregor didn't get away free. Knowing what she did, she suddenly felt responsible.

Another researcher who stood out, and was hard to figure, was Dr. Stull, the neuropsychiatrist. Superficially he was a pleasant person and Dr. Olmschied liked him, but his conversation was always so technical, always all business. He rarely talked about his wife and children, although once when he showed a picture to Cortney he seemed immensely proud, but to him every human emotion had a chemical basis—love, hate, depression, anger, anxiety, fear. People's bodies were conglomerates of neurotransmitters, he said. One's acetylcholine levels were either normal or not. Her morning blahs, as he once explained at breakfast, were caused by an underactive hypothalamus, and her excitement later by an accelerated reticular system. Nothing was subjective. Everything had a physical basis. People were machines, if very sophisticated, that regularly filled their fuel tanks with food rather than gasoline, and recorded information on organic computer tapes deep within their cerebral cortex. In fact, Stull's biggest joke was that man, acting like God, was now striving to make a robot in his own image, when he, in fact, was the robot.

Cortney tried to be friendly, mostly because of Dr. Olmschied, but sitting at the table with him made her feel distinctly uneasy—like a humanoid computer. If she seemed angry, he told her that the adrenal levels were flooding the blood-brain barrier and overtaxing her circuits. Maybe he was right. And maybe she was old-fashioned, but she still liked to think that there was *some* unknown element in man's mind that was unmeasurable, and God given. . . .

And then there was John Hicks. She couldn't help it, she did notice him. Everywhere she went, he seemed to turn up very soon thereafter—in the library borrowing books, on the observation deck, in the communications room, the exercise room, and even the arboretum, where she liked to wander to collect her thoughts and relax. Each time he claimed with a straight face that it was all coincidence . . . after all, it *was* a ship . . . but to her the encounters were clearly more often than the close quarters could account for.

Actually the problem wasn't him as much as it was her. She *did* find him attractive . . . superficially at least, his dark eyes, and many of his mannerisms, eerily resembled Michael's, but she'd come here to work, not play, and judging by his meaningful looks, he'd come to do both. Or at least it seemed, and her immediate reaction was resentment at being seen as a sexual object (still defensive Cortney).

He also had an uncanny way of showing up just when she especially wished he weren't around. Embarrassing times, like the first day in the laboratory. She was pushing the foundation to the electron microscope across the floor when her footing slipped. Twisting in a desperate grab at a cabinet handle, she missed and found herself helplessly twirling toward the ceiling. A moment later John came in, heard her and looked up to see this disheveled mass spinning on its own axis.

"A triple gainer ... ever consider the Olympics?"

"Just get me down," she commanded, starting her fifth revolution and getting dizzy.

"I don't know if I can," he said, stretching upward and finding that inches separated them. He quickly removed his Velcro sandals, pushed off from the floor and, feeling like the complete Superman, glided up next to her, where he grabbed a flailing arm. The stop was abrupt and as her face came around to his, it was very red from the increased blood flow to her head.

"Thank God, you came in when you did, although I guess I might have expected it." She saw the damnable grin on his face, and in spite of herself laughed at the absurdity of their situation, suspended as they were several feet off the ground, big deal scientists the whole world was watching, bouncing along the ceiling like two helium balloons.

When Dr. Olmschied came into the room a moment later and saw two bodies floating high above he remarked, "When the two of you finish doing whatever it is that you're doing up there, I could use your help down here, young lady."

Embarrassed, Cortney struggled down the wall to the file cabinet. "It's not what it seems," she started to explain, using the drawers as steps, when the security flap on the top drawer came loose and pencils, pens, and papers shot up into the air to smother her. John was barely able to get himself back down.

Half of Dr. Olmschied's experiment's protocol had suddenly become airborne, and he muttered in annoyed disbelief as he tried to recapture each piece.

Once all was again secured and John had left, they finally turned their attention to the monkeys. Nester had reported several problems to Olmschied, but most were minor ones that they'd anticipated, such as hoarseness and screaming and nervous skittering back and forth in their cages, but the amount of weight loss wasn't. Normally, a Rhesus weighs between fourteen and sixteen pounds, but few now tipped the scales at over thirteen. None were drinking and if allowed to continue, it could become serious.

After sedating each, Olmschied started an intravenous line to reinstill the lost fluids. Meanwhile, Cortney drew off blood samples for routine analyses. Everything checked, although the concentrated values confirmed the dehydration that was already apparent. White counts were normal, indicating that they were free of infection and normal red counts ruled out anemia.

"I don't think they're interested in each other except maybe to fight. None of them are lovers," Nester confided to Olmschied.

Olmschied shook his head. "Nothing short of a thermonuclear explosion would keep them apart at this time of the year. Maybe that's what they've really been screaming about."

"I'm not so sure," Nester said as he helped Olmschied return the animals to their new combined cages. One male and one female together in each.

In the adjoining room Cortney began setting up their monitoring equipment, the most important of which was the radio immunoassay for pregnancy. The hormone detection system was sensitive down to ten hours after conception and ninety-nine percent reproducible. Although mechanically complicated, the theory was simple: Once the fertilized egg touched the inner surface of the Fallopian tubes, minute hormone changes took place in the mother's body. By taking a sample of her blood, these hormones could be detected by interacting them with radioactive indicators in a test tube. If the value was elevated, the female was pregnant. If normal, it might just be a few hours too early. Other assays in the laboratory included an immunological analyzer for pituitary hormones—ACTH, TSH, FSH, and LH—as well as several types of estrogens from the womb to study fetal progression, a urometer to study the homone metabolites, and an ultrasonic holograph to visualize the fetus from conception to birth. The latter was an adaptation of the military's sonor equipment—using a specially designed transmitter-receiver (hundreds of tiny cups on a belt), inaudible sound waves could be bounced off the internal structures of the female merely by sliding the belt across her abdomen. Harmless and painless, it could project a vivid three dimensional image of the developing fetus as early as the second or third day of development. On earth the ultrasonic holograph, or U.H., was being used to detect early deformities so that a pregnancy could easily be terminated or rectified, depending on the problem. Specificity was down to ten days gestation, but Olmschied was hoping to get even better resolution. If any of these monkeys incurred a pregnancy with chromosomal abnormalities, it would be terminated immediately. The one thing he wasn't going to produce was monsters.

In addition to the portable devices, the laboratory had built-in monitoring devices along the outer wall—revolving graphs that recorded any cosmic radiation that might penetrate, where and at what time. Another machine situated in the animal quarters recorded temperature and pressure variations, while a third measured alterations in the carbon-dioxide-oxygen ratio. All very important variables that could affect the fetal development.

As the monkeys began to wake up now, Dr. Olmschied, Nester, and Cortney moved to a two-way mirror to watch, but the animals' first responses toward each other were far from loving. Instead, they fought, each issuing his own territorial imperatives and scrambling to protect the food he so far hadn't bothered to touch. None seemed sexually interested in the other.

Finally, when one female bent over in a show of submission, the male's thrust sent him rebounding off the opposite end of the cage. Angered, he charged again, only to rebound just as forcefully. Obviously confused, he gave up. This was one problem that Olmschied hadn't anticipated and one that urgently required a solution. For the moment, he didn't know what in the world it might be.

XV

November 11, 1991

AT 11:05 P.M. a policeman in Lewiston, Idaho, Howard Spears, and he was just coming off duty. He was worn out from a hard night's work and looking forward to bed. He was the only one in the parking lot and as he crossed toward his car, he loosened his holster. In ten minutes, he'd be home. Another five, asleep.

As he opened his car door and threw his hat and gun onto the front seat he heard a peculiar whistling sound. It seemed to be coming from every direction, and from nowhere. Along with it came a breeze, a cool, chilling breeze that ruffled his hair and gave him goosebumps. Standing outside his car, he stared at the homes across the way, down the street toward the traffic light and back up toward an all-night liquor store. Everything seemed normal. Except all around him the air was warming and suddenly it became unbearably hot. He looked up. A huge black mass was descending. Too late to unholster his gun. Too late to do anything....

At 11:20 two teenagers were clamming by lantern light along a deserted Oregon beach. With shovels in hand, they'd watch for a wave to slip out, spot the telltale hole bubbling, then quickly dig down for the elusive razor clams. Another half hour and the minus tide would be back in and they'd have to quit. But they only had one clam each, far less than their usual. Time was against them. They were so engrossed they didn't notice that the waves around them had suddenly flattened, that the usually bright starlight was blocked out and there were no reflections on the water. They were too busy digging even to notice that the air had become stale and warm. Too busy to know what happened in the absolute darkness that followed. . . .

At 11:45 a young couple was running from the surf off Venice Beach, California. Their naked bodies glistened from the beads of water, and both were laughing. The water was freezing, but they'd done it on a dare. Ten seconds was all that they could stand, and now they were hurrying back to their clothes to dry off. Neither of them noticed the hovering darkness, but both welcomed the warmth of the air. It felt good after the cold water.

The girl was the first to reach her clothes and as she jokingly picked his pants up and tossed them away, he tackled her and they fell to the sand in each other's arms. Around them the darkness increased, and soon after the lights of a nearby pier were obscured. The air became hot and as the girl opened her eyes, she screamed. It was too late, though. Too late for anyone to hear. . . .

XVI

"SHE STILL won't have anything to do with you?" Baumeister needled as he began scrubbing his hands with a series of specially impregnated antiseptic towels—the customary scrub sink and water used on earth was impossible at zero gravity.

John adjusted his face mask and took a handful of towels as well. "I think she's afraid a catastrophe's going to strike every time I come near her."

"You blame her?"

"I guess not," he said, ruefully shaking his head. He still had a vivid image of that exasperated look on her face at the end of their little free-floating scene in the lab.

"If I were you, I'd forget her. Don't even get involved. Women scientists are a special breed. I haven't met one that didn't have some . . . problem."

"Just looking for some diversion. The kind your ugly face can't provide."

"The only diversion you'll likely get from her is a professional dialogue. She probably doesn't know any more about sex than how frogs and planaria do it."

"Well, I'd certainly like to find out. And you shouldn't discourage my spirit of scientific inquiry. . . ."

But Baumeister was too preoccupied in upcoming business to reply. After changing to a second set of towels soaked in an alcohol derivative, both surgeons now carefully made their way into the operating amphitheater with hands held high and waited to be gloved in the customary manner. Working with them was Jimmy Ling, an O.R. tech whose main responsibility was the heart and lung machine, Mary Braverman, a nurse anesthetist who was sitting at the head of the table next to a calliope of gas tanks, and Rose Rutstein, a short, rather plump O.R. nurse who'd been with Baumeister for years. It was Rose who greeted them with sterile gloves and helped them into their operating gowns.

The operating room set-up was an exact duplication of Baumeister's dog laboratory at the university—white walls, a light green linoleum floor, no windows, a giant overhead spotlight shining down on the anesthetized canine and several glassed-in cabinets along the walls stocked with intravenous fluids, medications, surgical tools, drapes, and suture material. Under normal earth conditions a dog's body would remain stationary once gassed, but here, of course, it tended to float off the table. To prevent that, two leather straps were tightened across its abdomen and its legs tied to the table's edge. All surgical tools had to be magnetized, and although they tended to stick together they at least remained in the trays. Non-metal material such as drapes and sponges had tiny metal threads woven through the fabric, liquids had to be kept in sealed containers and all powders eliminated.

This first operation, an internal mammary artery implantation, was selected for its simplicity and the chance that it would give them to try out their equipment. It was a copy of a procedure done in the early 1960's in which the internal mammary artery, a long skinny blood vessel that traversed below the rib cage, was hooked up to the heart's own blood supply. Not only was the artery dispensable—other arteries could service the same tissues—but the additional blood flow to the coronary circulation often averted a heart attack. With the artificial heart, the procedure was largely obsolete, but for their first time out it represented a reasonable technical challenge, and if all went well, little harm would come to the dog.

The animal's chest was already shaved. After Rose prepped the nuded skin with more presoaked towels, Baumeister made the first incision with a high intensity laser. Like a highly polished scalpel blade, it silently cut a line from the base of the dog's neck to three inches below the diaphragm. When he was done, not a drop of blood was evident. Every severed vessel had been burned shut. After changing the angle slightly, he made a second slice down to the sternum, a glistening white bone that protected the heart beneath.

"Your turn," Baumeister said, looking up at John across from him. "Now we need a carpenter's hand."

John placed the circular blade of a rotary saw up against the breast plate, forced the guard in beneath its lower end and slowly cut up toward the dog's head. The procedure was tedious, but critical. A slip could easily send the blade down into the heart beneath, but as he cut he realized that the saw was much lighter and easier to handle than ever before. Thirty seconds later the bone was severed and they were ready to retract the ribs. The procedure required a device that resembled a reverse vise. Grasping the bone edges in its claws, they slowly pried the ribs up and away, some cracking beneath the pressure but most flexible enough to handle the strain. Beneath, they found a normal heart beating.

"Looks good. Everything stable?" Baumeister asked turning toward Mary.

"Vitals are unchanged."

After exposing the internal mammary artery and then freeing it from its muscular attachments, Baumeister made a cut through the pericardium, a semi-transluscent sac that enveloped the heart.

"There she is. Isn't she beautiful," Baumeister said as he proceeded to check his landmarks. Although each dog's anatomy was the same, occasionally there was a slight variation and this was the time to find out. Seeing that this dog was normal, he added, "It appears to be a piece of cake."

John had to agree. Nothing out of the ordinary had happened and it was beginning to seem that surgery here was at least as easy as on earth.

The next step was to prepare the artery—two clamps, cut in between and tie off the distal end. It was standard—but as John let loose of the vessel he saw the clamp now float upward with the artery in its teeth. Baumeister put on his magnifying lenses over his glasses and called for a pointed scalpel. Somehow, though, the metal clamp had shifted, and instead of hanging in space it drifted over toward John and stuck to one of his snaps. As John moved to give Baumeister more room, his weight tore the artery loose. In an instant the operating field was flooded with blood, huge spurts that coalesced into large red globules and blocked their view.

"Suction this out of here," Baumeister ordered Rose, who was doing everything she could, but the equipment couldn't keep up with the flow.

At the same time John reached down into the chest cavity to find the tear, but his vision was blocked and the injury was too deep to reach.

"Can you get it?" Baumeister asked, tossing the lenses aside and wiping the blood from his glasses.

"I don't know."

"Let me try," Baumeister said, pushing John's hand aside and digging into the pool of blood. Like a blind man reading braille, his fingers followed the normal anatomy back to where he felt a slight pulsation. Squeezing it between his fingertips, he watched to see if the bleeding lessened. The change was only slight. Forcing his way deeper, he squeezed again, and this time it finally stopped.

A kaleidoscope of red balloons floated about the room, and it took them several minutes just to vacuum the air and another half hour to tie off the injured artery. When they were done, Baumeister had had it for one day. Disgusted and frustrated, he angrily told John to close up, tossed his gloves in a nearby basin and stormed out of the room.

Piece of cake indeed.

XVII

MEANWHILE GREGOR'S experiment was going off without a hitch. To choose which twin from each set would undergo the artificial hibernation, a coin was flipped. Winning meant that the boy had his choice, and between the Simpson boys that was Dennis. Donald would remain awake beside him, acting partly as an experimental control and partly as a research assistant. Except for the actual freezing, the parameters would remain the same for both—weightlessness, radiation exposure, cabin pressures, lighting, etc. Using identical twins was like performing two different experiments on the same person in half the time—a researcher's dream.

The freezing procedure seemed simple, but every step was based on years of testing and every facet during the experiment monitored by computer. Assistants would be there to man the equipment around the clock.

Before beginning, the two "sleepers" evacuated their bladders and bowels. Then after receiving a mild sedative, a tube was run through their noses and down into their stomachs for mechanical alimentation, which was a menial two calories a day or the equivalent of a small slice of bread for a month. In fact, Gregor had considered eliminating this step for such a short period of time, but the Space Commission insisted on an exact simulation. Their astronauts, after all, would be flying for years.

Other monitors included a rectal probe to follow core temperatures, EKG pads attached to four spits on their chests to record heart rate and rhythm, wires wrapped through the axillae to monitor blood pressures and oxygen tension levels, and six electrodes distributed across their scalps to record brain waves. Each parameter was fed into a central computer, which in turn displayed the findings on a large television screen. If there was any change in their status, the abnormal numbers would begin flashing and if these alterations were serious enough to threaten either boy's health, the "hot gun" would immediately be called into play. This was a giant spotlight that rolled along a track in the ceiling and emitted an intense UV-infrared light. In an emergency, it could defrost each subject in less than thirty minutes.

Once the preliminary preparations were finished, the boys were moved into two cryobators, cryptlike structures whose walls were made of blue-tinted glass and whose base was a Styrofoam mattress mounted on the freezing machinery. For the moment both thermostats were set at room temperatures, and as Gregor checked the controls beneath, neither boy said a word.

The next step was critical. Using the antecubital vein in each boy, Gregor injected a phenothiazine drug to dilate their blood vessels. After their skins turned pink, he followed up with the preservative THEC, a thick, green solution. As it slowly flowed into their veins, their colors changed to an ashen gray and then blue-green. Both became comatose. The computer was set for a descent of one degree an hour, and the rest was already programmed in. . . .

Earlier in the morning, Dr. Olmschied had seen the four boys moving in profile through the corridor toward the South elevator. He could tell by their reticence that it was time for their experiment to begin and he felt deeply sorry for them. Cortney had told him about the leverage of gratitude that Gregor had so skillfully imposed on them . . . who could refuse when someone held the power of life and death over their closest loved ones.

The idea that a person would take advantage of another human being in such fashion infuriated Olmschied. Gregor reminded him of the Chamberlain family, who during the nineteenth century callously withheld the secret of forceps delivery from other doctors in order to enrich themselves. Eventually the family sold their invention for millions, but not before dozens of pregnant women and their unborn children had needlessly died.

Patents and copyrights had given Gregor the same opportunity—he was the sole proprietor of cryosuspension and could literally pick whomever he wanted to save, extract whatever price he wanted, and yet be protected by the law. To Olmschied, this was outrageous power unchecked.

Seeing Gregor had also intensified memories of his daughter. Before coming to the Space Lab he had expected that it might, but hadn't thought it would be so painful. The ten years that had passed since her death suddenly seemed like days. Once again he felt alone. And angry...she died a year after his wife had suffered a massive stroke and had to be moved to a nursing home. In twelve months time he had gone from a home alive with laughing to one that was wholly bleak and empty. He sold that home the day after and had never been near it since.

The leukemia that killed his daughter was one of the most aggressive cases anyone had ever seen. Usually the more active the cancer, the more likely there'd be a cure, but not so in her case. Her weakness progressed to where she could barely feed herself or roll over in bed, every bone ached and her body was covered with spontaneous bruises. A once beautiful, vivacious girl had disintegrated into a breathing cadaver who could barely say three words without stopping for a breath. Everything seemed helpless, hopeless, until Gregor offered to help.

At that time cryosuspension was still in its infancy, but Gregor was certain that he could forestall her death and possibly keep her until another drug could be found. Karen didn't want it. She pleaded with her father not to let the doctors do any more to her. There had been too many needles, too many nauseating medications, too many painful procedures. She wanted to be left alone, but Olmschied insisted that they try one more time. Gregor had reassured him that the procedure would be harmless and that all other leukemics had tolerated it well. He believed him because he wanted to, and it was only later that he learned that Gregor had lied. Karen was Gregor's first leukemic.

As she slipped into the hypothermic coma, her vital signs failed. Suddenly there was no blood pressure, and then her heart line was flat. Olmschied found himself standing there witnessing her death. Gregor tried everything, no question, but the rewarming process was too slow to help her. Later he speculated that Karen was too weak to handle the freezing, but Olmschied never forgave himself for forcing it on her, or Gregor for what had happened to her. . . .

As the boys disappeared into the elevator, he looked to his side and saw Cortney watching him. There were tears in his eyes, which he immediately said was an allergy attack.

Cortney offered him a tissue, not questioning his explanation, feeling certain that his mind was on his daughter.

The old man blew his nose. "We haven't got time for this. I've arranged for some diazepam from the pharmacy. I still think that we can get those monkeys to cooperate if we can just make them relax. Don't you?"

"Yes, I do," Cortney said, smiled at him and quickly followed him down the corridor.

XVIII

November 12, 1991

THE COLISEUM on Los Angeles's south side was quiet as Leonard Backus and Walter Jefferson, both maintenance men, moved their mops and buckets into a locker room glutted with mangled towels, dirty football uniforms, and muddy cleats. Neither man gave the mess a second look. It was typical. As Backus dunked his mop in the bucket, Jefferson began tossing the uniforms into a dirty wash hamper.

For Jefferson, this had been a more exciting night than usual. Not only had U.S.C. won with a last minute field goal but it also had netted him twenty dollars. Ever since, he'd been raving about one play after another as if he were somehow personally responsible. If the players were Trojans, they were all "my boys."

"Luck, just luck." Backus had lost the twenty. "If the other team hadn't fumbled on the fifty yard line, you'd be out of the money and a whole lot quieter."

"If, if, if. If they hadn't fumbled they'd have had to give it up anyway. If was fourth coming and long yardage. It doesn't matter, though. What counts is what's on the scoreboard when the gun goes off."

"Wait until they play Ohio State in the Rose Bowl. It'll be a slaughter. Want to go double or nothing?"

Jefferson started to answer, then hesitated. The sound of chains rattling outside caught his attention, and as Backus started to repeat his bet offer he waved him quiet.

"What is it?"

"I don't know, but I'd say we probably have us some kids up to no damn good."

Being partly responsible for vandals and yet hesitant to go outside alone, both men set their equipment aside and quietly walked out into the corridor. A moment later they

87

heard the chains again. This time louder, more violent.

"Awful noisy kids, don't you think?" Backus whispered. "Maybe it's just the wind."

"There ain't no wind tonight. I think we'd better have a look."

As they started walking in the direction of the sound, the corridor had become unusually hot and the air was stale. They figured it was their nerves working overtime.

They moved through the halls carefully, always turning the lights on ahead of them and checking side passageways. Nothing seemed out of order, and by the time they reached the gates the only sound they could hear was each other's breathing.

"Just wind, like I told you," Backus said, checking the padlocks. All were secure.

"I don't know," Jefferson said. Despite the barbed wire someone could have climbed over, and he said that they better make a trip around the stadium to be sure.

"You ain't going to find anything," Backus argued as he took a cigarette from his pocket and started to light it. As the match sputtered against the book, however, a tremendous gust of wind pushed him backward and blew out the match. "See, just like I told you. Damned wind." He got a second match, convinced that his point had been proved.

It was hard for Jefferson to argue. Even the gate chains rattled. Shrugging, he changed his mind about the inspection trip and started back toward the locker room.

"You goin' to give me double or nothing?" Backus asked, walking beside him.

"Double or nothing without any points? You just said it was going to be a slaughter. It's got to be at least seven points."

"No way."

"No points, no bet, but I'll be glad to take that twenty now."

As the two men made the last bend and started toward the door of the locker room, they heard a scream coming from behind them. Deep, guttural, it lasted nearly fifteen seconds. Both men froze. It repeated itself, louder, getting closer.

"What the *hell* was that?" Backus whispered. "It sounds like someone's being tortured or something. . . ."

"Some*thing* is right . . . that don't sound human to me—"

They heard footsteps coming their way. Footsteps, and an ear-piercing, monosyllabic scream.

Backus took off running. An instant later Jefferson was beside him, both men racing for the open doorway. They didn't know what was coming after them, but they were sure that they didn't want to see it close up.

When they reached the locker room they slammed the door shut and leaned against it, gasping for breath, drenched in sweat. Without a lock, they had no choice. Seconds later they heard the screaming outside and then there was pressure against the door. Pressure and pounding. They braced themselves, grimacing as they tried to hold the door tight shut. Whatever they were fighting seemed to grow angry with them at being opposed, but repeated slamming didn't budge the door.

"My God, what the hell is out there?" Backus said, slowly shifting one foot to a wooden bench to increase his leverage.

"I don't know but we've got to get some help," Jefferson grunted, and eyed a pay phone across the locker room. "You got any change?"

Holding his position, Backus dug into his pockets and came up with two nickles and a quarter that he gave to Jefferson.

The screaming and pressure had now let up outside, and as Jefferson slowly backed away to see what would happen, he asked, "Can you hold it?"

Backus nodded. There was no pressure at the moment.

Keeping his eyes on the doorway, Jefferson moved to the phone, dropped in the quarter and dialed the police. "Get a car, we need help, there's something outside. . . ." His words ran together, but he got out the word "Coliseum," followed by an abrupt crash. The door had caved in on Backus, flattening him to the ground, and in the doorway was a silhouette moving in. As it stepped into the light, Jefferson saw a ghostly white man, nude, hairless, with a raw surgical incision that ran from the top of his forehead down his face, splitting his tongue and on down to his genitals. Both parts of his tongue were moving as he screamed and screamed....

XIX

"WHY DON'T you just tie them together?" John suggested as he sat down next to Cortney and Dr. Olmschied in the dining room.

Both looked up in surprise.

"Nester told me what happened. About the trouble you're having getting them together and the tranquilizers putting them to sleep."

"And your answer is tying them together?" Cortney said. "That's crazy."

"I don't think so. You need something to give them some leeway but keep them from bouncing off the walls of their cages. Sort of a slingshot effect. If you want a horse to eat, sometimes you have to tie a feedbag around its neck. Same principle here."

"Eating's a little different than procreating, wouldn't you say? I doubt that any of the animals would stand for it, anyway."

"You know, it might . . ." Olmschied began. "Not the slingshot stuff. Tying them together seems a bit too much, but it gives me an idea."

Olmschied invited John to come along and the three headed for the hub. Nester had just finished feeding the animals, and he told the caretaker to put the animals back in their original cages. This time, though, there were to be two animals in the space provided for one.

"Instead of keeping them from bouncing off the walls, we'll just bring the walls closer to them," Olmschied said.

After the animals were safely transferred, everyone retreated behind a two-way mirror to watch. Standing beside them and peering through the tinted glass, John felt like a voyeur. At first, the monkeys seemed annoyed with their cramped quarters, crawling all over each other and screaming with discontent, but after a few raucous minutes the customary pecking order prevailed. That, *and* estrus. All three females willfully bent over in submission and the males mounted them. Ejaculation soon followed and John had suddenly become the hero of the moment. Olmschied was patting him on the back, extremely pleased that his experiment could now begin.

Ten hours later the radioimmunoassay for pregnancy was positive in two of the females, and by the next morning the test was confirmed in the third. As Cortney began running some of the preliminary tests that morning, John returned to see, he said, how the monkeys were doing.

"You'd think that you could walk on water the way the professor is carrying on about you," Cortney said looking up, and actually smiling.

John walked to the animal cages, stared inside at a monkey who was watching him with equal curiosity. "So you're going to be a papa." The monkey didn't budge, gnawing on something hard. Cortney came across the room. "Hardly. If you look closer I think you'll see that she's going to be a mama. That's papa in the next cage. We had to separate them."

"I guess that's why I'm a heart surgeon and not an obstetrician."

As Cortney laughed easily now, John watched, increasingly taken with her, and she, of course, was not unaware of it. Not displeased, she nonetheless changed the tone from personal to business. "Why aren't you doing your surgery?"

"The project's temporarily stopped. One dog's sick and we're waiting for some new equipment to come."

"And so with nothing better to do, you've been sitting around figuring out how we could get our monkeys to mate. You must have an interesting fantasy life, doctor."

"No more vivid than what you're doing here for real."

"You know, I suspect you're right about that...." Never mind the clumsy early approach, the embarrassments he'd caused her ... it was turning out considerably easier to be pleasant with him than in a running confrontation. She *did* like him...The ice had distinctly been broken.

They met in the dining room and talked some about their pasts, how their lives had abruptly changed coming here to the Lab...It was the first time in months that Cortney had found someone she could talk to so freely, and trite as it sounded in her head, it did indeed seem as if they'd known each other for a long while.

It was the same for John. He too felt the tension slip away, found he enjoyed *listening* to her. And then sometimes his mind shut out the words and he enjoyed even more watching her. Whatever Baumeister had said about women in science, he was clearly wrong about Cortney Miles. Not only was she wonderfully attractive, she was also one smart, well-trained scientist. And she was also a sensitive and caring woman...worrying just now in particular about Dr. Olmschied's health—was he eating properly, getting enough sleep, working too hard? It was as if she were mothering a man more than twice her age, but when John mentioned it, she looked at him and answered simply, "Look, he's a fine man—I don't care about age—and I happen to owe him. Okay?"

He nodded quickly that it was so.

They met that night and again the next morning. When they weren't working, they took to strolling about the ship, or through the fern forest, which was the closest thing to a garden with its dense greenery...No question in John's head that he wanted her, badly, but his more intimate approaches were always turned aside. By now she obviously enjoyed being with him, but it stopped at the conversation level.

He decided not to push. There was, after all, plenty of time.

XX

November 12, 1991

Time: 0845

GENERAL BOELLING stood up to greet Dr. Leigh as he entered the isolation unit at the U.C.L.A. Medical Center. Leigh, still wearing a sportshirt and slacks, had just flown in from Washington on a chartered military jet after being awakened in the middle of the night by an emergency call. "How are they?" he asked, shaking Boelling's hand. He meant the five bodies that had been found in the Coliseum and were now in the custody of the government.

"Don't know yet," Boelling said, sitting down as Leigh pulled up a chair next to him. The isolation unit was surrounded by guards and only authorized personnel were being allowed to come and go. "The doctors say they're all in shock, none has been able to tell us what happened."

"Must have been something pretty horrendous. What about the press?"

"So far, not a word has leaked. The police who responded to the emergency call checked their superiors first, and we've got the two janitors in rooms with guards. Whatever it was, it scared the hell out of them. If the press does get wind of something, the administrators have been told to say it's an exotic, virulent weed, very danger-ous . . . that some mountain camper must have brought it back, but that everyone exposed is in quarantine. If they've got to scare the public, let it at least be something earthborn—"

"Well, we don't know that it isn't yet . . . it might well just turn out to be some fanatical religious group—"

"I doubt it, we got a positive ID off of one of their fingerprints . . . a policeman from Lewiston, *Idaho*. He

94

only got off work two hours before they found him at the Coliseum. If he had wings, it would have taken him three times as long. *Something* damn well helped him."

"And the others?"

"Don't know much yet. They're too young for fingerprints to be reliable . . . one's a girl about seventeen, maybe eighteen. The others are boys around the same age. The police are checking missing person's reports now."

Boelling opened his briefcase and handed Leigh a series of photographs. On top was a distant shot of the Coliseum, but instead of the usually green surface, the playing field was brown with a huge black charred circle in the center. "That's how . . . they got here, or at least that's the mark left behind . . . just dumped out the bodies and took off again. No . . . there's no eye-witness to the craft. Radar at International didn't pick up anything, but the janitors did manage to mutter something about a big wind and hot air. . . ."

"There still might be some other explanation," Dr. Leigh said, but without much conviction.

"Believe me, I'd welcome it if you could find it . . . after you see these kids. . . ."

Leigh glanced up at Boelling. He'd never seen the General so worried. His own notions earlier that some other race of beings might be echoing their radio signals *seemed* like a plausible explanation, but deep down he didn't really believe it. Certainly didn't want to. Now, he was smack up against proof.

As he was studying the remaining shots, all different angles and different magnifications, a physician in surgical gown came in and Boelling introduced him as Dr. Stuart Kramer, Chief of the Infectious Disease Division.

"Have you gotten any more information?" Boelling asked.

"None of them can talk."

"Their tongues?"

"In part that, but they've all undergone a tremendous shock. They may never come back."

"What exactly is wrong with them?" Dr. Leigh said,

pushing the photographs back in their envelope. "All I've heard is that they've been cut up pretty bad."

"Cut *on* is more like it. Dissected. I think you'd better take a look."

Kramer took them into a special prep room to be sterilized by showering in an antibacterial soap and then baking in an ultraviolet booth. "We don't know if they've contracted anything yet, but we don't want to expose them to anything from us."

Next they were given isolation uniforms that covered their bodies and only left a small horizontal window for them to see through. The outfit reminded Boelling of an asbestos firefighter's uniform, only thinner and less bulky.

The room that they were taken to was a long plastic balloon with its own ventilation system. Inside, five bodies were laid out on stretchers. Each victim had a nurse attending them, with heart monitors blipping above their heads and intravenous bottles dripping into their forearms.

The first was the girl, and as Kramer pulled the sheet back and exposed the pasty white teenager, Dr. Leigh grimaced. There was a bright red incision transecting her abdomen as if she'd been cut in half, a second cut through her right breast and a third that made a complete circle around her forehead just above the eyes.

"Oh my God!" Leigh couldn't help the outburst. "Dissection" was indeed the appropriate word. Her incision reminded him of college biology class, except there the subject was a dead cat. . . .

As they moved to the second body, Kramer mentioned that the plastic sealant used in the incisions was unlike anything he'd ever seen before, and it seemed to hold much better than stitches. At least everywhere except the tongue. It had given way there.

The second body was one of the boys. He had three incisions—two down both flanks from his armpits to his feet and a third that began at the bridge of his nose and went straight back to the base of his skull.

Dr. Leigh had seen enough. He quickly left with Boelling and Kramer following.

"Now what do you think?" Boelling said, catching up.

"I *think* we'd *better* hope that this was done by some fanatical religious group," he said shakily, removing the uniform as soon as he got into the changing room, and heading for the men's room to throw up.

XXI

COMMANDER LYNDQUIST was asleep in his room when the bedside intercom began buzzing. Startled, he rolled to his side and slapped the receiver down. "What is it?"

It was Kreuger. "There's a meteor coming straight at us, sir. I just spotted it on the telescope. I don't understand, it seems to have materialized out of nowhere and now it's on a collision course with us—"

"What about the laser? Can you stop it with that?"

"I don't know. It's bigger than anything we've had to deal with before. The computer reads it out at ten times our size. I think you'd better come and take a look for yourself."

"How much time do we have?" Lyndquist asked, already starting to dress.

"Less than a half hour, maybe twenty minutes."

Switching to the channel for the command post, Lyndquist ordered Captain Thompson to sound a red alert and notify Mission Control of the possible collision.

A few seconds later the outer rim resounded with the alarm siren. Empty corridors instantly filled with personnel scrambling for assigned cubicles. The commander quickly made his way through the crowd to the East elevator shaft and fifteen seconds later was climbing into the plastiglass bubble with Kreuger.

"There it is." Kreuger pointed toward an innocuous appearing dot blinking in the distance. "It must be traveling at over a hundred thousand miles an hour. It's coming straight at us and I can't get a good fix to be sure."

Lyndquist studied the computations that the crewman had made, hoping to find some error and call off the alert, but all figures pointed toward a collision course. Moving to the telescope, he tried to assess the object visually, but details were difficult to make out. He changed filters to eliminate the glare, but that didn't help either. The best he could tell was that it looked like a distorted sphere. Probably a meteor.

"How soon can you shoot?" He meant the laser gun. Since the Space Lab was stationary, it was their only hope.

"Not for another fifteen minutes if you want to get anywhere near maximum effect. Otherwise we'd just be wasting power."

Lyndquist looked down at his watch. If Kreuger was right, they'd only have five minutes to deflect it. He switched to the intercom to be sure everyone was secure in the cubicles.

Every station was deserted except for the command post, where a skeleton crew held on. "We'll move out of here two minutes before impact," Thompson responded. "Mission Control says that crews for shuttle flights have already been called, but it'll be at least eight hours before the first ship can get to us."

Let's hope some of us are still here, Lyndquist thought, and automatically began reviewing the protocol for emergencies . . . and then realized he'd forgotten about the twins in Gregor's lab. They were still in suspension. Realizing he was closest to them, he descended the ladder and headed for the fourth level. Somehow he had to get their frozen bodies into one of the cubicles.

When he got there he found Gregor and the two awake twins moving the hot gun into position over the crypts.

"Didn't you hear the alert?" Lyndquist said.

"I heard it, but we've got to get these boys back first—"

"You don't have time. We've got to move them to a cubicle *now*." Lyndquist reached into the crypt and abruptly pulled his hand back. The intense cold burned him.

"The crypts can't be moved and neither can the boys. The only hope is to warm them. Thirty minutes, we'll all be in the cubicles." Gregor lined the gun up, attached a double-coned head and illuminated both sleeping bodies.

"Thirty minutes is too *long*. I'm sorry, you'll have to

leave them, there's a meteor going to hit this place like a nuclear bomb—"

"In that case, we'll all be dead and it won't matter. You go about your business saving the ship and I'll do mine."

Kreuger's voice came over the intercom to announce that the meteor was accelerating at an enormous rate and would be in firing range in a matter of seconds.

"Damn it, don't be a fool, get yourself out of here, and these boys to a cubicle. It's safer than staying here." And then there was no more time to argue as he headed for the doorway. Gregor, though, had tuned him out. The hot gun was working and the twins' temperatures were up ten degrees.

In Lyndquist's hurry to return to the bubble, he didn't notice that the door to the animal quarters was ajar. Inside, Nester was hurriedly gathering up the monkeys and dogs and putting them into small cages. He kept telling them this must be a drill and they shouldn't worry but he was going to move them to safety just in case.... The dog who'd been operated on, though, wasn't cooperating. When Nester picked him up and touched the incision, the dog nipped at his hand. As he pulled back, the animal got loose and began floating through the air, and each time Nester tried to grab him, the dog slipped away.

Meanwhile, the meteor had become clearly visible. It was moon-sized and cratered with huge pockmarks and deep ravines. Its course remained on a straight line toward the Lab, as if drawn by a magnet.

"Can you shoot yet?" Lyndquist asked, staring at it in disbelief.

The computer put the meteor at ten thousand miles. "Maybe, but it's a little soon. I don't know how much effect it'll have at this range," Kreuger said as he steadied the giant gun, set an electronic target finder and fired straight into the center of the mass. The power surge was barely adequate to reach its surface and only sent a few small chips flying away.

At seven thousand miles, a few more chips were

dislodged, barely enough to make a dent, and seeing the futility of it so far, Lyndquist ordered Thompson to leave the command post. Two minutes was about all that was left.

As Kreuger kept repeating his shots, probing for some soft spot or an angle that would change the meteor's trajectory, Lyndquist switched the intercom to Gregor's lab. The three there were still standing over the crypts and the wall unit showed that the twins' temperature had only gone up another ten degrees. "Gregor, get *out* of there," Lyndquist ordered him, but of course he didn't budge.

"Damn that stupid fool," Lyndquist muttered as he turned off the set. The cubicles were their only chance . . . and even with them he'd probably lose half his crew. According to Mission Control data the likelihood of anything this size even coming within visual range was one in a billion. A collision of any sort was supposed to be next to infinity, but there it was, homing in on them.

Nothing Kreuger tried worked. The meteor remained unchanged and the few additional chips he managed to knock away bounced like pebbles down the side of a mountain.

Finally he turned the gun toward the meteor's center, his finger still on the firing button. One minute to collision. The pockmarks had become giant craters, its rumbling sound was beginning to rattle the ship. . . .

"Get yourself out of here," Kreuger hollered to Lyndquist. "There's no point in both of us getting killed—"

Lyndquist wouldn't leave. Instead, he pushed Kreuger aside and took his finger off the firing mechanism. "We're going to give it one big try."

As they watched the voltage meter climb, the meteor's ugly face dominated the sky and kept coming, almost sucking the satellite toward it. One hundred miles . . . fifty . . . twenty. The laser had reached its capacity. At ten miles, Lyndquist aimed the gun into the belly of the largest crater he could see, pushed the button, braced for impact.

The laser's beam penetrated deep into the meteor's interior. Seconds later tiny canal-like cracks blossomed into monstrous canyons that split the meteor into four giant parts, which exploded off in different directions and barely missed the edges of the outer rim. They found themselves showered by a dense cloud of tiny, leftover particles that pinged against the exterior hull.

"You *did* it," Kreuger said, staring at the millions of light specks swirling across his radar screen. The change from the huge shadow to this was a welcome relief.

"That's as close as I ever want to come," Lyndquist said. He was hesitant to sound the all clear, though. Radar and visual were both blinded. Within less than half a minute his concerns were justified. Suddenly a tiny meteor, probably drawn by the parent's tail, Lyndquist figured, came rushing through the brown cloud, and before he could swing the laser around, smashed into the hub beneath them. The collision barely shook the bubble, but a moment later the lights went out and pressure began to fall.

Lyndquist immediately grabbed for a spacesuit and handed an abbreviated model to Kreuger. They could feel the air getting thinner as the oxygen meter indicated oxygen content was rapidly reaching the critical level. "We'd better get downstairs to help Gregor," Lyndquist said as he pulled the face mask down. If he's still alive, he added to himself.

Gathering up three extra suits from a nearby cabinet, the two men started down in the darkness. It was slow going, and when they reached the fifth level a flurry of papers shot past them and were sucked into the animal quarters. Beyond was a sizzling metallic ball and a monstrous window to the stars above it. Time was too critical to stay, but Lyndquist thought that he saw a man's body holding a dog floating outward into space.

The fourth level was in shambles. Gregor and the two boys were lying on the floor, cyanotic and gasping for air. The crypts had slid across the floor. Everything that had been knocked loose was slowly drifting upward toward the break.

Working as quickly as they could, they managed to get each of the three into spacesuits, adjusted the valves and then tried calling the interior for assistance. The intercom was dead. They'd just have to wait for help. Lyndquist immediately sealed off the laboratory to hold in whatever pressure remained, and then he and Kreuger turned to examine the crypts. The boys' skin temperature was still cold, and if they were breathing it was barely perceptible.

Gregor was slow to revive, but after a few minutes his eyes opened and he stumbled to his feet. Lyndquist tried to calm him, make him remain still and maximize the limited oxygen in his tanks, but he insisted on checking the boys. "We've got to take their temperatures back down. It's their only chance." He struggled to stand next to the computer panel and hit a button for auxiliary power. A moment later the panel lights came on, indicating the twins' life signs were near critical levels and any further warming at this time might be fatal.

"We've got to get them back down to freezing," he called over to Lyndquist, and started pulling one of the crypts back toward its original position. Still weak from oxygen deficit, he stumbled, gasping for breath. He couldn't gather enough strength to budge it. "You've got to help me, I can't afford to lose these boys. Not these boys, not this time. You've got to help me get them back down to freezing—"

"All right, just tell me what to do," Lyndquist said. Whether Gregor's motives were guilt or genuine concern he didn't know or care at this point. He and Kreuger quickly slid the crypts back to their proper places, then followed Gregor's instructions for the settings . . . the only way to save them, Gregor said, was to take them down much quicker than he'd ever tried before. They didn't have any choice.

For the next fifteen minutes they watched the life signs panel, keying in on every degree change, each millimeter of blood pressure change and every heartbeat. Although it had never been tried before, the faster method seemed as safe as the old way, and seeing that, Gregor felt more confident about his technique for the future. Accidents often led to major discoveries, he reminded himself with satisfaction.

By the time Captain Thompson rapped on the outer door, both boys were back down to freezing and resting "normally."

It took most of the night to resecure the fourth and fifth levels. Special heat retardant uniforms had to be used just to approach the meteor, a compact ten tons, and it took them two hours to pry it loose. Afterward aluminum panels were welded over the jagged entry and they could go to work on the interior.

Nearly everything in Olmschied's laboratory and Baumeister's operating room was gone, burned or melted. The walls were charred down to the basic foundation structure and all the animals were missing.

It wasn't until breakfast next morning that they knew for sure Nester was gone too.

XXII

November 12, 1991

Time: 2300

BOTH KITT PEAK National Observatory and Mt. Palomar simultaneously reported seeing an unexplained cluster of lights coming from the direction of Alpha Centauri. Altogether there were six objects that were traveling at speeds that approximated light, and all seemed to disappear once they reached earth's atmosphere. Initially the astronomers thought that they might be meteors, but a series of UFO sightings began occurring soon thereafter and each was consistent in time and description—a reddish-orange light, appearing about midnight.

The first official sighting occurred at Travis Air Force Base where radar picked up a strange blip that was hovering a mile overhead. Three fighter jets were immediately scrambled, but before they could reach the light it abruptly disappeared. A few moments later, the same thing occurred over Wiesbaden, Germany, and then London. In each case the jets were easily outraced, and when the objects were directed to identify themselves, the directions only echoed back.

Meanwhile, hundreds of unofficial sightings from around the world began piling up. Most seemed focused around military installations, but there were several over hospitals and universities, including Dr. Olmschied's school. Between two and three A.M. there were a dozen sightings by students while their car radios were echoing songs and TV sets had inexplicable double images.

By morning, newspapers were filled with stories about UFO sightings and many had pictures of the tiny specks in the sky. Although they were barely discernible, experts called them natural phenomena, possibly an offshoot of the Aurora Borealis, while the most imaginative speculated on them being precursors to an actual invasion from space.

The public didn't know what to believe. An elderly woman in Albuquerque said that she'd talked to three green creatures and convinced them to leave "us" alone, while a man in Toledo said he'd overheard two blobs outside their flying saucers arguing over the feasibility of raising humans on their planet for food. One had liked the taste, the other hadn't. In some places children were kept home from school that day, some people boarded up their homes, businessmen shut their shops and a good many crowded into their churches.

In Los Angeles the news media did learn of the five seemingly isolated cases, and when one of the reporters from the Los Angeles *Times* recognized Dr. Leigh, the hospital was invaded by reporters and TV crews. A scientist from the Space Commission, especially one of Leigh's prominence, immediately hyped speculation that these sequestered patients were victims of some extraterrestial forces. Dr. Leigh tried his best to discredit the notion, calling it old-fashioned science-fiction nonsense, adding as a topper that one of the virulent weed's victims was a relative of his, hoping that such a connection, however irrelevant on reflection, would somehow lend weight to his disclaimers. The reporters weren't buying, and when General Boelling was also identified, the clamor for information intensified. Space science plus military...?

Dr. Leigh felt he really couldn't give them more. Yes, incredibly there was credible evidence of some sort of "visit," but they didn't actually have proof. For him to publicly acknowledge the possibility would cause a panic. He could do no better than repeat that these patients were victims of legitimate *earthborn* diseases. Period. Boelling went along, and said he was in Los Angeles on his way east to Washington and had dropped in to see the professor, an old friend. Weak, he realized, as did the press.

That night, after most of the reporters had gone, three Army helicopters set down on the hospital's roof and moved the five victims to Camp Pendleton. Everyone remotely involved in their care was taken along.

XXIII

Dr. Olmschied, sitting alone at breakfast next morning, was depressed and disgusted. In front of him was a cup of coffee. His appetite was gone. There were always things that might go wrong in a research project, but this was beyond his calculations. His equipment was gone, the animals lost, and worst of all a man had died. The likelihood of resuming the investigation seemed bleak, and he wasn't sure that he'd ever want to anyway.

When Dr. Baumeister came into the dining room and joined Olmschied, he seemed unreasonably cheerful. He too had lost everything, and yet his spirits were high. He was particularly interested in Olmschied's plans. "What now? Back to square one?" he asked, diving to a full tray of food. It was obvious that his appetite had not been affected either.

"Maybe next year. The estrus period is just about over—"

"Why not skip square one entirely and go straight to number one hundred or even one thousand. Whichever you choose." The surgeon dumped liquid salt over his eggs.

Olmschied wasn't following, and found himself distinctly annoyed by the surgeon's unaccountable good spirits.

"I've been giving your work a lot of thought ever since I got here," Baumeister went on. "Obviously neither of us can continue as planned. The way I see it we either come up with an alternative or start packing for home."

"I've already begun," Olmschied said as Gregor entered and approached his table.

"Sorry to hear what happened," the Stanford professor offered in apparent sincerity, then added, "but did you hear how fast we got those boys back down. My process should work in a matter of minutes, don't you think . . . ?"

Gregor's enthusiasm was met with a distinctly sour look from Olmschied, and even Baumeister, and he removed himself awkwardly to another table.

"I think we ought to come up with an alternative project," Baumeister repeated when he'd gone.

"There *is* no alternative, not until next year. At least not for me."

"Not so, doctor. Together we have the perfect experiment. It's as I mentioned to you the first night... I've been giving it thought ever since. After all, the world won't be sending monkeys out to colonize the universe. No matter what you show in the laboratory with primates, the work will eventually have to be done with *people*—"

"When we're ready, not before."

"Those are your rules, not necessarily anyone else's. You've been trained to follow a special progression, but this is nearly the beginning of the twenty-first century, research has changed. You've already laid all the necessary groundwork. The monkeys proved conception can easily occur and that the fetus remains viable—"

"There's a big difference between viable and healthy. The hunchback of Notre Dame was viable."

"But you can always abort the fetus if something goes wrong."

"It's not quite that easy," Olmschied said, annoyed. He really didn't feel like debating his work. Not now.

"The effects of radiation are probably less here than on earth—"

"And weightlessness?"

"Men have survived longer than nine months under weightless conditions. A gravid female might have some additional problems, but that's what we have to find out."

The "we" was not lost on Olmschied. Baumeister, the preeminent opportunist, was already seizing what he saw as a bonanza opportunity. "I'm afraid you're wrong!" Olmschied's voice rose. "There are too many changes in the distribution of bodily fluids. Blood shifts from the legs to the thorax and abdomen, skeletal tissues break down from disuse. Who can say what effect these will have on a pregnant woman. We don't even know what it would do to monkeys, whose gestation period is considerably shorter. No sir, it's got to be monkeys first, and thoroughly studied—then, and only then, humans!"

Baumeister hesitated for a moment. He could see the professor heating up, and although he was determined to do the experiment alone if necessary, he wanted Olmschied's participation. "You do realize that anyone could do the work...."

"I doubt it."

"All one would need is two healthy, uninhibited volunteers. In fact, it might happen here on the Space Lab, say among the crew, without ever consulting you or any of your electronic gadgets. And meanwhile Dr. Gregor's work will be finished in only a few months and you know how he'll trumpet his success and diminish your experiment and mine—"

"Over that I've little control, and less interest in," Olmschied angrily responded, and started to get up.

"You could have a good deal of control if we teamed up and worked on this project together—"

"That's impossible!"

"Or ... I could even do it alone."

Olmschied stared at the surgeon a moment. "Yes, I imagine that you could, and you can also go to hell without my help."

As Olmschied hurried out of the dining room he passed John and Cortney just entering. She started to speak but his expression quickly froze her. He continued past them without saying a word.

Turning to follow him, she persisted, "What *happened?*"

"The man's a thief."

"Who?"

"Baumeister."

"Why?"

"Ask him. I'm sure he can hardly wait to spell it out." He headed straight for his room and slammed the door behind. Cortney, left outside, decided that whatever was bothering him had to be something other than the loss of their project or Nester's death. He'd be depressed over these, not angry at Baumeister.

She quickly went back to the dining room and asked Baumeister what had happened. John had already joined him.

"Just a friendly disagreement between scientists—"

"It hardly seemed that way to me. I've never seen him this mad."

"I'm sure he'll cool off and we'll all sit down and talk it out . . . why don't you get yourself some breakfast?" He seemed to be looking at her intently, and it made her damned uneasy.

"Discuss *what* later?"

"At least sit down, we've already attracted enough attention." Baumeister pulled a chair out for her. "All right . . . here it is. His work is ruined. So is mine, right? I merely suggested that we pool our resources and collaborate on an experiment so that the trip would not be a total loss for both of us."

"What kind of an experiment?"

"Reproduction in humans. . . ."

"Without fully studying monkeys first?" Cortney's thoughts naturally paralleled her mentor's.

"As I see it, there are only two options here. Either he waits for another year or he goes ahead with humans, who can, after all, conceive every month. Not this once-yearly business with estrus. The work could be done under his same guidelines . . . I've already cleared it through Lynd-quist, I spoke to him last night. He says that they can have the labs functional in a week or so. Olmschied can run the entire show, I'll just stay in the background in case he needs a surgeon . . . to do a cesarean or an abortion."

Cortney felt like saying How nice of you, but held her sarcasm. What was to be gained? But she could understand now why the professor had stormed out. She felt like it herself. Never mind that Baumeister's intrusion into their work was a monumental presumption, with the implicit threat to steal it, it was a dangerous step to take without the preliminary work, just as Olmschied had said. Calming herself, and hoping to encourage a reasonable accommodation, she said, "Why don't we wait until we're all back home and then talk it over—"

"And miss this unique opportunity here?"

John had been quiet long enough. His colleague's excess was also getting to him. He sided with Cortney. "She's right, doctor. It's really Olmschied's area. We can bring up some new dogs and go on with our work—"

"No. John, I'm surprised at you . . . this can be the most important experiment of this century. I mean it. Without Dr. Olmschied it may be difficult to do, but *not* impossible—"

"You wouldn't," Cortney said, stunned by his open challenge.

"If I don't, someone else surely will, and it won't be Dr. Olmschied. I can guarantee you that. I hoped I wouldn't need to say this, but I see no alternative . . . I happen to know that the Commission was planning to bypass the monkey experiment and go directly to humans when the professor pressed the issue. I doubt very seriously that they'll reconsider this step again and wait another year to get it started. I also know that they almost didn't allow him to come because of his age. If they send a second team, he definitely won't be a part of it."

"They wouldn't do that, not to him," Cortney said, and afraid as she protested that indeed they might.

"You ask him then."

Cortney decided to do exactly that. When she arrived outside Olmschied's room, however, the professor refused to respond to her knock.

"I'm staying here until you let me in," she called out, knowing that he was inside but not aware that he'd just taken two nitroglycerins for his chest pain.

Moments later the bolt clicked, and she saw as he retreated back to his cot that his face was very pale.

"Are you all right?"

"Of course." He waved her off. "I suppose he sent you here to convince me to—"

"He didn't send me here to do anything. I came on my own and I need some answers."

"Such as?" Olmschied lay back, dropping his head on his hands. "Can we sue him if he goes ahead with my experiment? Can we sabotage it or send another meteor into the laboratory?"

"He says that he wants to work with us."

"Don't believe it. The man's an egotist, like Gregor. They're two of a kind. Gregor lied to me, prematurely experimented on my daughter and killed her. Now Baumeister can't wait to do another experiment on humans without decent preparation. People like this, they don't belong in the profession... God only knows what will happen... The man smells some glory and the scent has gone to his head. The artificial heart wasn't enough. Not for him, He craves a topper."

"But what if he goes ahead without us anyway? Then where are we?"

"Back home, and at least with guilt-free consciences. He says it would be done with two crew members. Unscreened, who knows what genetic problems there'd be.... No, I'll have no part in it. We can come back next year and do our work properly. His efforts are bound to be... incomplete. We'll have to pick up the pieces and go on—"

"Will there be a next year?" Cortney was sitting on the edge of his bed.

He looked at her curiously. "Of course."

"He doesn't think so." She took a deep breath. "He says the Commission won't let you come up here again."

Olmschied looked stunned. He'd gotten the message. O'Hara's words about his heart went through his mind. He tried to evade the issue. "A misunderstanding, that's all. A misunderstanding. They didn't understand my proposals—"

Cortney noted the small bottle of pills in his pocket and

took them out. "They're not going to let you come back here, are they?"

"I don't know." Olmschied's tone was soft, almost resigned.

"Then I've decided for us. We're staying."

"*You*'ve decided?"

"Yes, I've decided. I'll be the subject you need. My genetic profile's clean, you said so yourself. And I'll absolutely need you here to monitor me and be sure I'm okay...."

Olmschied's beginning protest was cut off by the door closing behind her as she quickly left his room.

It was an offer he hated to accept. And one he knew he couldn't pass up.

XXIV

AT FIRST it was almost the same for John. He'd hoped to convince her to be intimate with him, then had all but given it up, and now she coolly announced that she planned to have intercourse with him "purely for scientific research purposes...personal feelings aren't involved, we'll do what is necessary...." Personal considerations were subjugated to test tubes, electric wires and oscilloscopes. Terrific.

Too many lonely hours had gone by since his marriage ended, but to perform for machines and statistics...still, when he thought about it, there wasn't any logical reason not to go along, just an uneasy, intuitive feeling. And there was the fact that she'd picked him....

Dr. Olmschied's reluctance hung on, but with Cortney's persistence he finally agreed. With one stipulation—if they were going to create a child, he needed to study John's genetic profile as well. At least in this way the infant's health would not be jeopardized by a preventable disease.

The test that he performed was the same he'd done on Cortney years before—a tissue biopsy, the chromosomal breakdown and genetic dispersal, all done in one of the undamaged laboratories. Altogether it took him two days, but when he was finished John's results were remarkably similar to Cortney's. His life expectancy was approximately ninety years, and none of the major categories showed any significant diseases. If they'd been superstitious, it would have been easy to assume they were "destined" for each other.

In addition to the genetic profile Olmschied requested a specimen of semen. When John protested, the professor insisted. They'd do this his way or not at all. He handed John a sterile bottle, pointed him toward an empty room.

Results were good. His count exceeded three million sperm per cubic centimeter, the motility pattern was normal and there was only a rare trace of aberrancy. Olmschied had hoped to find a reason to cancel the experiment. So far there was none.

Meanwhile Cortney set about checking her own hormone levels to determine the exact date of ovulation. Usually she'd experience a telltale twinge of pain in her lower abdomen about the middle of the month, but this time she wanted no guesswork. Since her period had just ended, it only gave them about ten days.

Baumeister's job was to secure new equipment, and since the experiment was his idea Olmschied insisted he use his own funds. "You wanted this, you can at least pay for it." The surgeon had millions to draw on and he very little. A shopping list was drawn up, which Baumeister ordered his hospital staff to get to work on immediately. Within a few days most of the needed items were on their way.

Meanwhile Dr. Olmschied's old laboratory was converted into living quarters for Cortney. The walls were repainted, the wiring and ventilation systems revamped, burned and melted equipment moved to one of the storage areas. The room was still a metal cubicle, larger than her room only along the outer rim, with a vertical sleeping bag for a bed and a sealed plastic booth for a shower. Meals would be carried from the kitchens. An open line of communication with the command post was installed. Other than the two crewmen in the crow's nests and the twins from Gregor's experiment, she would be alone at night. It looked like—and in its fashion was—a prison cell, and her sentence was nine months.

As they waited for the right day, neither John nor Cortney spoke of the actual 'event.' They pretended to ignore it. One day she'd be living in the outer rim, the next she'd be pregnant and living in the hub. Cortney seemed to be adjusting herself, at least she didn't show the strain on the outside. John was still bothered. But each time he

even started to approach the subject, she diverted him.
She wanted to hear no arguments.
She wasn't sure she could resist them.

XXV

November 18, 1991

Time: 1200

AN EMERGENCY Joint Chiefs of Staff meeting was called at the Pentagon to review the sightings, work out a strategic defense should the earth, and in particular, the U.S., come under general attack. These were, of course, contingency plans. No one actually knew what they were dealing with.

Aside from the Coliseum episode, which was still being investigated, the evidence for any outside presence was still flimsy. Few of the sightings to date came from reliable sources such as pilots or astronauts, and most of the generals still believed that they were dealing with a form of mass hysteria. Everyone and their brother was seeing suspicious lights in the skies. Commercial airlines could barely leave their runways before someone reported them to the Civil Defense authorities and cloud reflected spotlights were being shot at. H. G. Wells all over again, and anything that moved in the night had to be extraterrestrial.

Still, the generals' job was to protect against eventualities, whatever their opinion. How to defend against "them" if they indeed existed. If it was true that they could fly at speeds equaling light, most of our weapons were useless. Only the laser guns were a possibility, and they only numbered a half dozen on each coast and hadn't been tried in combat. They could call up the reserves and cancel leaves of the standing army, but there didn't seem real purpose in shifting personnel around. With an enemy coming from above, the attack could occur anywhere.

XXVI

ON THE thirteenth day of Cortney's menstrual cycle, John was sitting alone in the observation room, staring out the earth-side porthole, which was where Baumeister found him.

"It's time," the older surgeon announced, and at least, John thought, resisting the impulse to say anything personal. "Cortney reports her estrogens are over 60 units, the progesterones are beginning to appear and the egg has entered her right Fallopian tube. She can feel it."

"Estrogens are up, progesterones are closing fast ... sounds more like a horse race." He felt considerably less funny than he tried to sound. He was, he realized, scared.

John started to stand, then hesitated. "I'm not sure that I can go through with it—"

"You *can't* back out now, not after all we've done. No one's asking for a commitment. Do it and leave."

"That's just it, I don't think I can. I feel like some damned stud service. Worse, I don't really believe her heart's in it as an experiment either—she's doing it for the old man—"

"So what. She's an adult. So is he. No one forced them to stay."

"You don't really believe that, do you?"

"They could have taken the next shuttle back. They're just as interested in doing this experiment as I am. But if you're not willing to participate, I can always recruit someone from the crew—"

"Even you wouldn't—"

"I'd do anything to complete this project. It's the ultimate experiment before colonizing space, and we're in a position to complete it. It's *important* scientific research. Just pretend, my boy, that she's one of those glass containers Olmschied gave you."

Good lord...for the first time John could see how desperately ambitious Baumeister was. His feelings toward other humans were as cold as his scalpel, and as direct. In his fashion he'd managed to coerce the professor and Cortney into doing this, and now he was doing the same to him. He was clever...damn him...John didn't doubt for a minute that Baumeister could and would recruit volunteers if necessary, and he'd probably get away with it. So he couldn't renege. The experiment was degrading enough for Cortney...without a word, he left his chair and started toward the elevator shaft. As Baumeister started to follow, he turned. "The least that you can do is contain your voyeurism and stay here."

Throwing up his hands as if to say no offense, Baumeister stopped and stared, but as the doors to the elevator closed, there was a smug look on his face. He'd won.

Olmschied was at his workbench in the adjoining room when John entered.

"You have any preference...about how we go about this?" John asked.

The professor looked up, lifted his glasses from his nose. "The same way, I imagine, that men and women have been going about it since time immemorial."

John allowed himself a smile. It was the first time he had in days.

He entered Cortney's room. The lights were dimmed. She was lying beneath the covers on a bed. Her shoulders were bare, her face expressionless. Not a word was said between them as he struggled in the weightlessness to undress and then, silently, made his way to her bed. She lay there as if in a trance, as though trying to force herself to be unresponsive to his presence.

For a moment, he sat by her side, touching and then stroking her hair. Her eyes were trained on the ceiling. She didn't move. He wanted to tell her that he was miserable or that he loved her, but how do you tell someone you're miserable before you're intimate with them, and the genuine feelings of love just weren't there, however much he wished that they were. He wanted to say that it would be all right, how could he when he was far from sure of it himself, knew how fatuous that would sound. And what about the child? What if it weren't normal? Or even if it were, would it be *theirs?* Or would it belong to science, a curiosity... and have to go through life with the knowledge that it was borne to test an hypothesis...?

Pulling the covers back, he saw her breasts, the cool air making her nipples stand erect. Like a mannequin, though, she stayed motionless. No foreplay. He was to do it expeditiously as possible, wait for the results. An experiment. Very scientific. Damn it... it was all too mechanical... and then aloud, "I can't, I just can't... this isn't right, not for you, not for me, and especially not for an unborn child...."

Cortney finally looked at him, unbelieving. Here she had given herself without a protest. Her body was his, for the moment at least, no strings attached, and yet he, not her, needed the consoling. But then she could see the unmistakable anguish in his face, and felt a rush of compassion... more than that, of caring. They'd built something, after all, during all those hours of confidence together...

"This child will be loved, by both of us," she told him, moving her hands up to caress his face. For a moment they lay in silence, neither of them sure of the other's feelings, both seeking some reassurance.

"I just don't know," John said, looking into her eyes apologetically. "Maybe—"

Cortney drew him closer to where their bodies touched. She moved his arms up to embrace her. A moment later, they kissed. At first hesitantly, then lovingly.

"I still—" John began again.

Cortney quickly clapped her hand over his mouth. "Do I have to tie you to me to get this done," she said, surprising herself with her earthiness, and John let out a burst of grateful laughter. A second later he'd kicked the covers free so that their bodies could float upwards, and soon they were tightly entwined and rhythmic.

When it was over, they slept in each other's arms, somehow convinced that a child had been conceived, and out of love.

The date was November 13, 1991, one day before the President's speech.

XXVII

THE NEXT morning Dr. Olmschied drew a specimen of blood from Cortney's arm and an hour later confirmed that conception had occurred. Both Cortney and John were tremendously excited. Their feelings toward each other had changed, apparently overnight, but not really, just the open expression of them. They'd become potential parents. John was even talking about having the commander marry them, "to make things legal," but Cortney remained the more restrained of the two and wanted to wait. She liked him, of course, but her feelings were short of making a permanent commitment. For the moment, she wanted more time.

Despite that, John was beside himself with the news of the baby. One of his fantasies had finally come true. In time-honored traditional fashion, whatever she wanted, she was sure to get—something to eat, to drink, a book, cookies, whatever. He made a half dozen trips to the outer rim, already bragging to himself about his child-to-be. He still despised Baumeister for his pressure-play, and yet he now almost wanted to thank him. And laugh in his face.

Dr. Olmschied also seemed pleased, especially when Cortney asked him to be the child's godfather. He quickly accepted, after all he was partly responsible too, but being a natural skeptic he restrained his enthusiasm...there were still too many variables ahead to be dealt with, not to mention the old feeling common to all good researchers that things might not go as expected. And he had, after all, lost one child already. He didn't want to pin his hopes on another that was less than a day old.

Meanwhile, Dr. Baumeister was in the communications room setting up a press conference—an international press conference. He wanted the world to know about the baby, and within minutes the wire service stories about UFO's were scrubbed for those about the baby. Representatives from all major news organizations hurriedly gathered inside Mission Control. By noon they were set to go.

On the other end of the hook-up, however, was only Dr. Baumeister, beaming like a man who'd first conquered Mt. Everest. Neither Olmschied nor John were interested in exploiting the event to the media, and Cortney, an unwed mother involved in a "sex" experiment, certainly didn't want to be put on display.

"Why are you so interested in reproduction at this time?" a reporter asked.

"Man will conquer the stars, it's only a matter of time," the surgeon began with a well-practiced flare for the dramatic. "He can only do it by *colonizing* the universe first. Distances are too great, and travel still primitive. Someone has to show that reproduction is possible. It's much like earlier flights when eating and drinking had to be tried to see if they were possible. If not, we couldn't have proceeded. Now, it's time to check reproduction. Nothing can be assumed. My colleague Dr. Olmschied was a pioneer in this field and now we're reaching the endpoint."

"This is quite a change for you, isn't it?" another reporter asked. "We were under the impression that you were doing heart surgery and Dr. Olmschied was studying reproduction."

"After the unfortunate meteor accident, Dr. Olmschied asked me to assist him. The ground work had been established that reproduction was safe in monkeys and now that he was shifting to humans, he needed another physician to help him. Much of the credit goes to him, but we hope to make a contribution in some small way ourselves."

John was watching on a remote video set, feeling sickened by Baumeister's fake humility.

"How's the mother doing? Can you tell us about her?" a

woman reporter asked.

"Well, it's early, you know, but so far she's just fine. She's in good spirits and her health's excellent. She's a brave young woman to have undertaken this project—"

"How long will she have to remain in the center hub? Will she be able to come and go?"

"No, I'm afraid for the sake of the ...experiment...she'll need to remain there for the full nine months. If we're to study the full effects of zero gravity, she must stay. But I might add that she's a willing participant...." (John turned his set off and went back to the hub. He'd heard enough.)

"What about the father?" the reporter followed up.

"He can come and go as he pleases. We're interested in the effects of outer space on the fetus, not on him."

"Is there anyway that we can speak to either of the parents or Dr. Olmschied?"

"Not now, I'm sorry. Perhaps later."

"What tests will you be running?"

"Most are a bit too technical to describe, but the fetus will be evaluated daily through the ultrasonic holograph, there'll be daily blood and urine tests on the mother, that sort of thing."

"What if something goes wrong?"

"There's no reason to think that things won't go well. We're professional optimists. All scientists have to be."

"But what plans have you made if they don't?"

"...Contingency...." Which was to say, nothing.

"Have the parents picked out any names yet?"

"It's only sixteen hours old. It's only two or three cells along in its development—"

Lyndquist interrupted the broadcast, saying this was all the time that they could allot. Baumeister promised periodic news releases with updates as well as more conferences. He was going to maximize this project for all it was worth. To him.

After the commander had changed the video frequency, he turned to Baumeister. "This ought to make more headlines than our solar transmitter did."

Baumeister, well-pleased with himself, said, "Well, commander, sex has always been more interesting than light bulbs, otherwise so many people wouldn't turn them off first." The commander wanted to throttle him.

XXVIII

THAT NIGHT, while Commander Lyndquist was waiting for the President to begin his televised speech, an urgent call came from the command post. Captain Thompson reported that the radar screens were picking up another unidentified object, rapidly coming in their direction. Kreuger hadn't made visual contact yet, but it was expected momentarily.

Lyndquist left as the speech began...

"My friends and countrymen, there is a growing disease across our country of epidemic proportions with fears such as I've never seen before. People are afraid to leave their homes after dark, children are sent to bed afraid of the morning, and life itself in this country is losing its quality of vitality and optimism. Everywhere I look, I see faces that are afraid, afraid of the so-called unknown. Now let me tell you, there is no provable cause for such alarm...."

When Lyndquist arrived at the command post he ordered the area sealed off to everyone except authorized personnel. He'd already been briefed by secret communique about the UFO's and been told to keep any encounters top secret. As he stared at the scope, it was undeniable that *whatever* this was, it was coming altogether too fast to be man-made. The computers put it at 200,000 miles per second, too fast even for a meteor, and when he checked with Kreuger, he was just picking up a reddish blur in the distance.

"I don't think it's a meteor, sir, but it's right on course for us again," Kreuger said as he relayed the image down to the command post.

"How much time?"

"Two minutes. Should I sound the alert?"

"Hold for a second, but get the laser gun ready." Lyndquist then quickly changed channels for Mission Control and General Boelling.

The commanding officer was in the receiving room at the time and immediately advised him not to engage in any hostile maneuvers. "There's no evidence yet that they're dangerous, but if they get too close fire a warning shot."

"They"...? As Lyndquist debated on sounding the alert, the opportunity to shoot never came. The object started slowing at one hundred thousand miles out and at ten thousand started circling the Lab. Everyone in the command post remained quiet, but in the background they could hear the President still speaking....

"There have been UFO sightings on record since 1949. Twenty thousand cases that we know of and another fifty thousand that we estimate never reached our files. Ninety percent have been fully explained: planes, helicopters, balloons, clouds, reflections, pranks; ten percent have not. Of these that remain, many have been described exactly the way these reports are coming in. Now, if we assume that we've been seeing them for over forty years, and not one person or one country has ever been attacked or harmed in any way by them. Too many people, I'm afraid, are telling too many stories and scaring the daylights out of themselves and others. I urge you to...."

The channel to Mission Control was kept open, with a video image of what they were seeing in the Lab—a blackened disc-like object that circled first one way and then another, never getting closer than ten thousand miles and yet viewing the space lab satellite from every possible angle.

Finally after several minutes of silence, Lyndquist decided to make contact. As he began, his voice sounded unsteady. He realized he even felt a little foolish. "This is the commander of Space Lab Five. Please identify yourself and state your purpose."

Seconds later, he heard his own voice returning... "This is the commander of Space Lab Five. Please identify yourself and state your purpose." He wanted to believe that it was an echo, but the delay had been too long.

"Our purpose here is scientific research. This is a peaceful mission," Lyndquist resumed, assuming now that "they" or it or whatever the hell were hearing him.

"Our purpose here is scientific research. This is a peaceful mission," came the response, word for word and inflection for inflection.

Shutting the transmitter off, he turned to Thompson. "They're *duplicating* everything I say," and a few seconds later they heard..."They're *duplicating* everything I say," in the commander's same whispered voice.

"Let me try from here." Boelling broke in..."This is General Boelling from Mission Control on earth. Would you state your purpose and your intentions."

"Let me try from here.... This is General Boelling from Mission Control on earth. Would you state your purpose and your intentions."

"This is *crazy*," Boelling muttered, then repeated, "please state your intentions, are they peaceful?"

"This is crazy, please state your intentions, are they peaceful?"...

In the background the President was still talking. "Suppose for an instant that I'm wrong, that we're being watched by little green men with long antennae and fifteen toes on each of their five feet. Why haven't they made contact before? If they exist, they're obviously afraid of us. And rightfully so. Our lasers should be able to track any of these lights, and I'm assured by the military scientists that these...things, if indeed they are even entities, cannot escape the laser beam's range...."

And meanwhile, the "disc" kept circling back and forth outside the Space Lab, never changing, never veering from the chosen ten thousand mile orbit.

"What now?" Lyndquist asked.

"Try the emergency channel," Boelling suggested as soon as Lyndquist's echo disappeared.

The change in channel, however, was no improvement. Not only were they picking up their own conversation, but ones from the turbine room, Hydroponics, the laboratories, and lastly the President..."So there you have it. A no doubt natural, if as yet unexplained, phenomenom that had been with us for a very long time, and may even continue to be. . . . I don't know about you, but I'm going to bed. I suggest you all do the same."

As the President stood up to leave the Oval Office, he was handed an emergency top secret communique. It was a message from Mission Control that a sighting had been confirmed and the disc-like ship or whatever was still hovering about. Instead of going to bed as he'd said, he called for another emergency Joint Chiefs meeting.

This time their plans were not to be contingency.

And meanwhile, the object continued its orbit for two hours, sampling conversation from all over the space lab, then broadened its loops, and left.

XXIX

By the fourth day of gestation, the ultrasonic holograph began picking up an image of the developing embryo. As expected at this level of magnification the projection wasn't entirely clear, but by carefully manipulating the tiny receivers across a lubricant on Cortney's abdomen Dr. Olmschied was able to demonstrate the morula stage—a rounded clump of sixteen cells that resembled a miniature raspberry. He was able to watch it move from the edge of her Fallopian tube to the back wall of her uterus, where it was beginning to implant. It was impossible, though, to tell if any of the cells had begun differentiating into definite types, but the embryo's external appearance was altogether normal. So far at least, human conception in space appeared to be safe.

Cortney seemed pleased with the pictures, and asked the professor if he could tell if it was a boy or a girl.

"I don't think the cells know themselves yet. I'm only sure it'll be one or the other."

Actually the full impact of being pregnant hadn't hit her yet. All of the tests said she was and the holograph confirmed it, but under normal circumstances she never would have suspected it. There were no outward signs—no morning sickness, no food cravings, no mood swings. She felt exceedingly well and, with it, was convinced that the next nine months in waiting would be easy.

That quickly turned out to be not quite the case. Her first night alone in the hub, lying vertically in a sleeping bag, tied in so she wouldn't float away, staring out at the stars, she was suddenly afflicted with a backlog of reservations. She had sailed into this so-called experiment, not allowing herself to think how she and the professor had, in effect, been duped by Baumeister. Did she do it out of affection for an old man fighting to stay

131

alive professionally—and, in his case, personally—a man who had been enormously kind and supportive...? Was she even capable of being a *mother?* As a scientist, she could pretend to be an observer for nine months, but what about after that was all over? If only she didn't have to stay in a dark room and listen to the walls creak she might feel better, but the experiment's protocol required that....

She didn't sleep well that night... she loved John, no, she didn't, it was too soon to know, she'd be a loving mother, no, she'd never really thought about having children and didn't know how she'd be... she even hoped that something or someone would end the pregnancy, relieve her, and at the same time she wanted the child to survive unharmed. She wished that she was married... conventional Cortney... and she was glad she'd decided to wait. As a scientist, she thought that this was a great experiment; as a woman, she had her serious doubts. Suddenly there was a third party, an unborn participant, and no one had asked his, or her, opinion....

By morning she'd made up her mind to see this through. She'd love this child just as she told John she would, and she'd do everything in her power to see that it did well....

Daytime was easier for her. Someone was always around, she had books and magazines. Soon telecommunicated mail began arriving. Most was congratulatory, wishing her and the baby good health, but a few were condemnations. Science had legitimized the illegitimate child, they said, and her loose morals would not be imposed on the world under the guise of the research. She tossed out the critical ones, saved the others.

Usually a fairly shy person, now she directed a barrage of conversation at whomever walked through her door in the morning. The lonely nights had increased her appetite for company. Olmschied would not be distracted in his work, but John was very willing company, staying later each day, the two of them chattering on about childhood memories, ex-romances, hamburgers with blue ketchup, outer space grocery stores that would stock edible coca-colas...it all bordered on the absurd, but it helped keep her sane.

Meanwhile John also worked out an exercise program for Cortney to counteract the effects of prolonged weightlessness and to keep her body generally healthy as possible. Each morning she had to spend an hour running on a conveyor belt, and every evening she would stand in a special suction machine to keep the blood from leaving her legs and pooling in her thorax and abdomen.

John and Olmschied worked out a special diet that was high in protein and carbohydrate, low in salts. It was barely palatable, but other than an occasional crinkled nose Cortney didn't complain. With John's help she'd become increasingly determined to see this through.

On the fifth day Olmschied was able to pick up a microscopic cavity within the morula where the cells were differentiating into two separate groups. The inner cells would eventually become the embryo while the outer cells would transform into a placenta. The differentiation was right on schedule, and as the connection between mother and child became more evident, nutrients began traversing the primitive umbilical cord. Before that the embryo was functioning on its own reserves, but now it would have total support until the day that it was cut.

On the sixth day John was sitting alone in the observation room. His eyes were on a passing Space Tow Truck, a heavily boostered rocket that was pulling a small Asteroid back to earth for mining purposes, but his thoughts were on the newly conceived child...a boy, he hoped.

Intermittently a worried thought about the weightlessness would intervene. It was still an unknown and couldn't be discounted. What if it caused the child to be retarded, or crippled? The thought that it might have been prevented would always, literally, haunt him. He didn't want to think about it. If he did, he knew he'd drag Cortney away from the hub, and that was something he couldn't do.

His thoughts were interrupted by a conversation between two crewmen entering the room. They were talking about a UFO sighting and they'd come to the observation room to see if they could catch sight of another.

"*What* UFO?" John asked, abruptly turning to face them.

Both men seemed surprised to see anyone there, but having been sworn to secrecy by Lyndquist, neither wanted to answer him.

"I said, what UFO?" If there was any possible danger to the Lab, or anyone in it, he damned well had better know about it.

"Just kidding, sir," the higher ranking crewman said, and his friend quickly nodded in agreement. "We run low on joke material out here."

"You sounded serious to me."

"Oh, no sir."

To John, their responses sounded forced, although he realized that ever since he'd gotten the news that Cortney'd conceived, he'd been worried, edgy . . . the baby and she had become his family, he their protector.

Still, the crewmen's conversation stayed with him, and that night at dinner when he found the commander sitting alone he decided to draw him out and joined him. Lyndquist seemed pleased to have company and immediately asked about Cortney.

"Mother and child are doing well. . . . You have children?"

"Used to. Grown up now. Even a grandchild."

"How old?" John seemed and was surprised to hear that Lyndquist was old enough to be a grandfather.

"Three and a half. Just getting to that age where he'd enjoy seeing one of these satellites. He already has a dozen models in his room."

John nodded . . . "Incidentally, have you guys identi-fied that UFO yet?"

"What UFO?"

"The one you were tracking the other day."

"How do you know about that?"

"I don't," John said, feeling considerably more worried. "I happened to overhear two of your men talking. What's this about anyway, and why haven't you told the rest of us?"

"There isn't anything to tell." Lyndquist returned to his food.

"I find that hard to believe. If there's any danger, we all should know about it—"

"I can't tell you any more than you already know, this thing's top secret."

"I don't give a *damn* about top secret. The government can't play games with peoples' lives . . . I want to know exactly what the hell is going on."

Lyndquist stared hard at John for a moment, then seemed almost about to respond when a crewman interrupted to say that the commander was urgently needed in the command post.

"Another alleged sighting?" John asked.

Lyndquist started to deny it, then changed his mind. "Why don't you come along and see for yourself. They say a picture's worth a thousand words."

When they arrived at the command post an orangish-red disc-like object was being magnified onto their viewing screen. Thompson located it ten thousand miles out and indicated that it was beginning to circle the Lab "like the three before it."

"We've been seeing about one a night. They come in a variety of colors, all too bright to see beyond the lights," Lyndquist said as he turned on the radio receiver. The voice they heard was Gregor's. The scientist was repeating a series of vital signs to one of the twins. "That's not Gregor you're hearing," Lyndquist said to John. "I know it sounds like him, but that's *them*. They repeat almost everything we say around here. That is, everything except conversation around the turbines. The noise there apparently drowns them out." Lyndquist picked up the microphone and handed it to John. "Want to try your luck. See if they'll talk to you. I've given up."

"I don't think so," John said, stepping backward, looking at Lyndquist in disbelief. His voice, though, carried over the radio waves, and seconds later the words "I don't think so" came echoing back.

"We know that they can hear just about everything going on inside here, and I sometimes wonder if they can't see inside too. Maybe it's just my galloping paranoia—"

"For God's sake, can't you *do* anything about it?"

"Mission Control says to sit tight, so we just sit here while they check us out." Lyndquist turned the dial to a different channel. "Gary, are you there?"

"Affirmative," came a voice from Mission Control.

John couldn't believe this. Flying saucers, echoing voices, unidentified for real objects ... like watching a science fiction movie, or living one.

"At least they don't seem to want a confrontation, but no one seems to know what their intentions are either. So far they seem content to just look us over."

While Lyndquist was speaking, "they" continued their echoed eavesdropping in particular on Gregor, and the professor's calm changed to one of abrupt concern.

"Something's wrong with the crypts," one of the twins said. "They don't seem to be getting any power."

"It must be a loose connection somewhere ... the computer's fine ... but their temperatures are starting to rise. They're *warming*...."

Lyndquist switched to the video intercom and saw the professor rushing between the crypts.

"Nothing's wrong with the computer, it must be the crypts."

"It's not the crypts. Two machines don't shut down at the same time and have nothing wrong with them," Gregor said, shifting to the computer again. Before him the vital signs were flashing as usual, but everything he tried failed. "I just can't take this again."

Lyndquist immediately switched to engineering and ordered a team up to help.

"You think that thing out there is responsible for this?" John asked.

"Let's hope not."

Lyndquist left the command post and headed toward the elevators, John close behind. By the time they'd arrived the professor was in a near-frenzy. His computer panel was flashing alarm lights, the boys' temperatures had risen dramatically and one of his assistants was pulling the hot gun into place. "If they don't come back to normal in a controlled manner, the change will kill them," Gregor nervously said.

Superficially, it seemed no more than that a fuse had blown. But when they tried plugging other electrical appliances into the same outlets, they worked. Using extension cords to the other labs also failed, and when Gregor dragged in his back-up unit—a smaller but equally competent crypt—it too wouldn't start.

Whatever was wrong obviously was inherent to the crypts alone, and the critical point for initiating proper retrieval methods was quickly approaching. Gregor signalled the boys to warm up the hot gun, but an instant later there was a fizzling sound, a pop, and then nothing. The gun too was dead.

"That *can't* be. There's too many things going wrong at the same time. Too many coincidences," Gregor said, and then seeing Olmschied standing in the doorway, added, "unless someone's trying to sabotage my experiment—"

"I doubt that very much," Lyndquist cut in as he bent down to examine the inside of one of the crypts.

"Well, there's some around who'd try to destroy my work...."

The computer's alarm system indicated they'd reached the critical point, and a decision to refreeze or rapidly warm them had to be made. In spite of the alarms Gregor began pacing back and forth, muttering to himself.

Lyndquist finally grabbed him by the shoulders, shook him. "Dr. Gregor, get a hold of yourself." But the professor's eyes seemed glazed over, his mind stuck in the wrong groove.

Seeing that he was really incapable of making any decision, Lyndquist looked to Olmschied, who now approached the crypts, studied them for a moment. "Get me some ice. Get me all the ice you can find on this ship and start making more as fast as you can."

Gregor's eyes moved to Olmschied as he grabbed a wrench. He started toward him. "*You* stay out of here. Stay away from my children, they're resting, I don't want them disturbed—"

Before Gregor could get halfway across the laboratory John caught him, took the wrench away and pushed him back toward the wall, where he slumped. "I think we'd better get him out of here," he said to Lyndquist, who nodded and signalled to two of his men.

Within a few minutes several buckets of ice were thrown on top of the warming bodies, which were then wrapped in blankets to keep the cubes from melting too quickly. It took a while for their temperatures to reverse, but finally the alarms stopped sounding and everyone took in a deep breath of relief. Nobody was clear about what to do next, but at least they'd bought some time.

They focused on the inner workings of each crypt, inspecting every inch of wire, every connection, every transistor. Nothing was explained. They seemed in good working order. They didn't work. . . .

"Our only option seems to be to bring them back slowly as possible and hope that their bodies can acclimate to the changes," Olmschied suggested. "Once I was very familiar with the process, but that was years ago. . . ." He didn't explain the reason for that familiarity was his daughter, that before allowing her to undergo the cryosuspension he'd read every scrap of available literature he could find, but at that time the journals were sparse, since most of the information was still in Gregor's head. . . .

Still, despite whatever knowledge he lacked, he did recall that bringing them back very slowly at least sometimes worked, so each hour small amounts of ice were removed from the crypts and lukewarm water dripped in. Every degree of change was monitored—every heartbeat, every breath—and each time it appeared as if they were progressing too quickly, the ice was re-introduced.

Time inched by as Olmschied meticulously monitored every change. Of course he was helping a man whom he despised, but that was hardly the issue now ... these boys' lives were all that really mattered ... Perhaps in some way, he thought, his efforts now would compensate some for having allowed his daughter to undergo an untested hypothesis. He'd been helpless, then, but maybe now. . . .

Meanwhile John had made a special trip to Cortney's room to tell her what had happened and use it to convince her that she, her unborn child, could be in danger too and that he wanted her to leave on the next shuttle flight.

"How bad are they?" Cortney asked, her eyes barely open and bothered by the bright lights.

"I don't know. Olmschied's been working on them. Gregor's under sedation, and useless. He seems to have snapped. I want you to get your things together and forget this whole crazy experiment. You can spend the night in my room—"

"No ... I'm not leaving just because Gregor's experiment is in trouble." She got out of her sleeping bag and gathered a robe around her. "You think they need me down there? I'm sure I can help the professor in some way—"

"I don't think you should go and I doubt Olmschied would want you there. We still don't know what's wrong and there's no need exposing you and the baby needlessly—"

"To what?"

"I don't know. Toxins, radio waves. Who knows ... look, I want you to listen to me for once and—"

"You're not making any sense. I'm going." She started toward the doorway.

John moved in front of her. "Please, honey, just take my word for it. Stay away from Gregor's laboratory and come with me, I'll explain later."

"There's something else isn't there? Those boys are already dead?"

"No, they're not dead."

"Then, what is it?"

He obviously couldn't avoid the issue any longer. "There's a...UF...hell, some sort of flying saucer or some damn thing outside this lab...that somehow it's responsible...."

Cortney began to laugh. "Did I hear you say, *doctor*, that there's a flying saucer—"

"Yes, damn it, you heard me—"

"And you think that it's sending down some mysterious ray that's affected Gregor's experiment?"

"I don't *know* what I think, but I assure you it's not too funny—"

"But that's absurd. Good lord, we used to see flying saucers out on the farm every year, and I assure you that not one of them ever aimed their ray guns at us."

"Like I said, this is not funny, those boys might die and we don't know why—"

"Listen to you," she broke in. "I think you've gone batty. I'm going down there to see if I can help."

Short of physically restraining her, John couldn't stop her, but when they got to Gregor's lab Olmschied exploded. "Why'd you bring her here?"

"I assure you I didn't, she insisted—"

"*Just get her out of here.*"

Cortney started to argue but Olmschied repeated himself even more forcefully and went back to the work at hand.

"Now will you listen to me?" John asked as she finally turned to leave.

"No, not until I know more about what's going on here," but she did go back to her room, where she stayed up the rest of the night waiting for news about the boys.

Progress was slow, but twelve hours later the boys began to come awake. They were groggy and sick to their stomachs, but alive. Olmschied called for stretchers. Once they were stable, he had them moved to Dr. McLaughlin's infirmary. It wasn't until he climbed down from his observation perch that he realized how overwhelmingly tired he was. He stopped by Cortney's room to apologize for his outburst, told her that the boys would make it and headed for his own room. It was the worst strain he'd undergone in years—mentally and physically.

Outside, the hovering object was gone. Thompson fixed its departure at precisely the time the boys were brought down. Soon afterward they found the crypts wholly functional once again.

XXX

NEWS OF the human reproduction experiment on Space Lab V spread around the world, outdoing the publicity given to the UFO's. Some of the more restrained newspapers featured such flat-out headlines as "BABY TO BE BORN IN OUTER SPACE," followed by a description of the Ceres project and a background on John and Cortney, while the more sensational offered such as "SEX IN OUTER SPACE" and "COUPLE MAKES LOVE FOR SCIENCE ON SPACE LAB."

The media once again descended on the Space Commission offices and Mission Control.

Dr. Leigh was all but trapped in his office. And whenever he did manage to go out for lunch or left for home reporters followed, demanding to know details, about Cortney and John, when was the baby conceived, what . . . yes, it was the most persistent question . . . were they going to name the baby, as though this was the most important issue in the whole affair. Dr. Leigh thought of the old French saying, "The more things change, the more they stay the same. . . ."

General Boelling, after the first day, packed a bag and moved into Mission Control. Everything that he needed was there, and now, with the confirmed sightings by the Space Lab, he felt he had to be close at hand for whatever might develop.

Public reaction was mixed. Like the reporters hounding Leigh and Boelling, people wanted to know more, but . . . multibillion-dollar space probes and research satellites were acceptable, but for some experimental fornication was stretching it a bit. Religious groups, in particular, objected, the scientific community approved, Congress sat on the fence.

Meanwhile the findings at the Coliseum remained a well-guarded secret, and the two janitors stayed in custody. The evidence uncovered seemed conclusive that the five victims had been kidnapped by an extraterrestrial ship, were surgically "examined" and then dropped off. Apparently "they" wanted to learn more about the human species—each subject was missing a part of his or her body—the policeman, the frontal lobes of his brain; the clam diggers, a stomach and one lung; the girl, her uterus and ovaries; and her boyfriend, one kidney and part of his liver. Although the incisions were technically perfect, all five remained comatose from shock. Police records in each state revealed no more than that they were still missing persons.

XXXI

NEITHER THE outside disc-object nor Gregor's disaster nor John's importuning changed Cortney's mind. Admittedly, the idea of being around flying saucers, or whatever, in space was distinctly unnerving, but mysterious lights and echoing voices were not enough to send her packing, not after committing herself to a pregnancy...She argued that the so-called UFO would have attacked their food supplies or destroyed the oxygen stores if it really meant them any harm and that Gregor's accident had to be because of some kind of electrical interference, something that would never apply to *their* experiment.....To her, it just didn't make sense that this...entity, whatever, it was, would single out Gregor and leave the rest of the Space Lab satellite alone. No...she was sticking.

John finally had to agree with her arguments, but not her apparent equanimity. They were dealing with a total unknown, and being so far from earth, were extraordinarily vulnerable. On earth, they'd be one of a crowd; here, they were prime, pinpointed targets.

During the next week he made numerous trips daily to the command post to check for new sightings, but always found the registry empty. "They" had disappeared as abruptly as they'd come, and Lyndquist was even able to joke, "We either scared them off or disgusted them." There were also encouraging negative reports from earth.

He couldn't, though, leave it alone so easily. They... it was still hard to characterize whomever, whatever...must have come to look us over, and now by their absence were hopefully showing they were convinced we didn't represent a threat. Why else come? Our technology by comparison had to be primitive, and if so, there was no need to harass us. Or so he lectured himself....

Dr. Gregor and the two sets of twins had left with most of their equipment, leaving the back-up unit and a few accessories for the next flight. With a little help from Dr. Stull and a long acting tranquilizer, the scientist did manage to regain most of his composure, but never made an effort to thank Olmschied. The two scientists resumed hostilities as if nothing had happened, and as Gregor departed he promised that, like the famous general of World War II, Douglas MacArthur, he would return.

By the beginning of the third week Cortney was starting to feel the early effects of her pregnancy—first subtle changes such as increased fatiguability and needing more breaks during her exercises but soon the hormone changes were affecting her stomach...thought of food sickened her and everything she forced down found its way back up.

She was also becoming depressed, sick of the same walls and the daily tedium. Sometimes she felt like a prisoner in solitary confinement, and snapped at John's attempts to cheer her up.

Everyday at 0800 and again at 1700 Baumeister made a trip to Cortney's room as if he were going on normal hospital rounds back home ... he'd enter the lab, check her charts, ask how his girl was doing. She'd give him some curt answer, something she knew he'd want to hear, he'd say something reassuring and take off. It was all abbreviated and impersonal. He was their medical adviser, but John, with Baumeister's blessing, made most of the medical decisions. Baumeister had never reconciled himself to the "premature" nature of the experiment, and how he'd been forced into it.

By the sixteenth day the holograph showed that the placenta had firmly established itself and the embryo was taking on the appearance of a flattened egg within a fluid cavity, the amniotic sac. The embryoblast cells had differentiated into three major tissues: the ectoderm, which would eventually play a role in the formation of skin and nerves; the mesoderm, which would develop into muscle; and the endoderm which, would form most of the internal organs. Though still miscroscopic, the primitive stage was set.

And yet despite the normal progression of events, Cortney seemed to be worsening. Each day she felt a little sicker, and soon was refusing to eat or drink anything. Instead of gaining weight, she was actually losing, and finally John stopped the exercise program out of fear that she might hurt herself.

Her appearance scared him. Her complexion was pasty white, her eyes had deep circles under them. Instead of welcoming him around her, she told him she wanted to be alone and her moods shifted from one extreme to another. One moment she'd be laughing, the next, crying hysterically, and neither made much sense in the context of the immediate situation. Angry outbursts became the rule, and when she on one occasion overheard Olmschied telling John that they might have to terminate the pregnancy if she got any worse, she started calling him a murderer and throwing everything within reach at him.

By the twenty-first day her condition had deteriorated further. Refusing food and water, she had *lost* some ten pounds and was refusing to allow anyone to run any tests on her. Olmschied tried reasoning with her, no use. She was, frankly, irrational. Finally, worried that her life might actually be in jeopardy, he called a special meeting in the conference room. Dr. McLaughlin and Commander Lyndquist were included.

"I think it's time to abort the pregnancy," the professor began once everyone was assembled. "If we don't stop this now, the damages to Cortney may become irreparable. I don't think she can hold up much longer like this—"

"Don't your think that you're being a little extreme, going so quickly for an abortion?" Baumeister argued, seemingly unconcerned. "We see this kind of reaction with lots of pregnancies—"

"She looks a good deal worse than most I've seen,"

John said, his heart sinking at the possible necessity of an abortion. Still, if it truly came down to a decision between mother and child, he'd without question favor an abortion. He wasn't sure, though that they'd reached that point yet.

"It's all just some morning sickness plus fatigue," Baumeister insisted. "The poor lady hasn't been sleeping, even though she's exhausted. A circle. Weightlessness may be complicating things some, I suppose...." He looked to Lyndquist. "Isn't this what you see in your own men who aren't accustomed to zero gravity?"

"Not exactly, but they get a little sick to their stomachs." The commander wasn't too keen to get involved in this decision.

"I for one am flatly against an abortion at this time. I think it'll pass," Baumeister declared, as if the meeting could now end.

"What about the baby?" McLaughlin asked, looking toward Dr. Olmschied. "I haven't heard anyone say a word about the baby.

"The last time I checked, it seemed to be doing very well, although that was some days ago. There was normal maturation, normal size, normal activity, and parts of the brain and kidneys were evident. At the moment I'm not sure—"

"The baby's health is not the issue here," John interrupted. "What we're concerned about is Cortney."

"And *I* say they're both fine," Baumeister said. "We'll sedate her, hook up an intravenous line for a few days and she'll be as good as new again."

"Can you guarantee that?"

"No, of course not, but my experience tells me that you're all being a bit hasty here—"

"Well, what about Cortney?" McLaughlin asked, "has *she* been consulted about having an abortion?"

"Not formally," Olmschied said. "She's not exactly in full control right now, I doubt she'd be able to give a rational response."

"Then it seems to me that you don't have a choice.

Unless a court finds her incompetent, you can't force an operation on her. At least not in my book. Or on my ship."

His argument seemed the most cogent. Even if they were certain that her life was in jeopardy, which they weren't, the final decision, they agreed, still had to be in her hands. And so seeing that further discussion of termination was futile, Dr. Baumeister outlined a therapeutic approach and the meeting was concluded.

XXXII

AFTER CORTNEY was sedated, an intravenous line with a combined protein and emulsified fat solution was inserted in her left arm. Unlike on earth, where gravity caused the fluid to drip, they used a special pressure apparatus to force it downward. The infusion rate was set at one hundred milliliters per hour (the equivalent of a quart and a half of water in twenty-four hours), and someone was contantly there to keep watch. For the most part, it was John.

The next day he moved all his belongings to Cortney's room, and Lyndquist arranged for an extra bunk to be installed. Whenever he was sleeping or needed a break, Dr. Olmschied or Baumeister spelled him, but by the end of the second day he could see at least one reason why Cortney was having trouble. The room was just too confining. If he didn't take a few minutes to get back to the outer core and walk about in freedom, he too became irritable from claustrophobia.

In the meantime daily fetal measurements were resumed, and despite Cortney's weight loss the fetus appeared to be doing well. By the twenty-third day the oral and anal membranes were present, and by the twenty-fourth a tubular heart wrapped in a gelatinous casing. The embryo had now progressed from its earlier circular body to one that was almost an hour glass in configuration, bulky at both ends with a narrow groove down its back.

On the twenty-fifty day Cortney began to improve. Her color returned and with it her arms and legs regained some of their lost strength. The wide mood swings disappeared and in their place she became amicable and easy to please. For John it was an especially gratifying change. Much as he hated to admit it, it seemed Baumeister was right.

Later that same day Cortney was able to keep liquids down, first broth and tea and then pureed vegetables. It took an additional day before they were convinced she could maintain her own nutrition, but once she was eating a regular diet the intravenous line was discontinued and she was allowed to start walking again.

Having been bedridden so long, the first steps were the most difficult. After each step, her muscles cramped and John had to help her balance. If not for the weightlessness, she probably couldn't have walked at all, but together they pushed, walking back and forth in the room, and later when Olmschied lifted some of the restrictions they exercised in the corridor. Her progress was slow, but steady.

With the pleasures of pregnancy returning, they began to consider names for the baby. A boy was easy. As the first born in space, it would have to be Adam, but Cortney definitely was against Eve for a girl . . . it reminded her of an old maid Latin teacher of hers, an ornery vicious woman. But none of the other names they considered fitted—too common or cute or self-consciously different. It would just have to be a boy.

At night John stayed at her side, even though the intravenous line was gone. This was where he felt he belonged. This was his family. Cortney was part of his life and he of hers. Whatever problems she had, they were his now as well. They ate together, slept together, made love together. But as for marriage, Cortney still wanted to wait, to be absolutely sure, but her refusal no longer sounded as definite as a month ago. John was beginning to hope. . . .

It was late evening of his third day in the hub. Cortney had just fallen asleep and Dr. Olmschied was working at his desk when the man silently slipped by and entered Cortney's room. John, who'd been reading, looked up in surprise and trying to keep his voice down, asked the crewman what he wanted. The man's embossed name on his uniform said Meyers. John couldn't recall ever having seen him around the hub before.

The man's angry response was loud but barely intelligible. It woke Cortney.

"Is there something wrong? A leak in the pressure?" John said, assuming that he was one of the maintenance men, and a damn rude one at that.

The man ignored him, walked past him and looked over their equipment. He was obviously upset, his forehead was drenched with sweat.

"What's this all *about?*" John said, and when the man didn't answer, he started toward the intercom. "I think we'd better call the commander and find out why you're here." But as he crossed the room the crewman blocked his way, standing fast and glaring at him.

"I think you'd better let me through—"

The man grabbed his arms and squeezed.

"What the *hell* do you think you're doing?" John demanded, trying to free himself, but the man's grip was like iron. He tried kicking and twisting to break the hold, and was promptly hoisted into the air and thrown against the wall. Cortney screamed, and a moment later Olmschied came rushing into the room.

"What's going on, who are you?" the professor asked in rapid succession, and found himself talking to a stone wall—a stone wall that was moving toward him now, wide-eyed. He started to back away. The crewman lunged at him, grabbed hold of his arm and whirled him over toward John.

"What do you *want?*" John said, looking for something that might serve as a weapon.

"I want this experiment to cease. . . ." The man's voice came in a monotone. "Breeding people in space is against His will . . . you were instructed to reproduce and multiply on earth, not here . . . it will bring you pain and death. . . ."

After surveying the room again, the crewman left silently as he'd come. His eyes never blinked, his expression never changed. It was as if he were in a trance.

Moments later John had the commander on the intercom, who quickly was out in the hub talking to them.

"I can't believe it," Lyndquist said, immediately

recognizing the name. "I doubt he'd have the slightest interest in what you're doing—"

"Well, he gave a pretty good imitation of it, and he's dangerous," John said, feeling shooting pains down his back to remind him.

"If it's the Meyers I'm thinking of, he's a mild sort, hardly a religious fanatic, no one here is."

"Dark hair, brown eyes, about thirty," Olmschied gave a description for confirmation. "And his right sleeve is torn. I saw it rip when he threw me—"

"That fits the description, but I can hardly believe it." Lyndquist suggested he and John talk to the man, to confirm identification and to try to find out *why* . . . If he was the one, he had plenty of explaining to do.

Leaving the hub, they went straight to the command post to check the worksheets, but Meyers was listed as off duty. "He could be anywhere," Lyndquist said, then, noting the hour, added that they should try his room first.

They took a security guard along and headed toward the crew's quarters. When they arrived outside Meyers' room they found the door slightly ajar and its lock broken away.

"That's pretty strange," Lyndquist said. "It looks as if someone broke *out* rather than in."

The room was dark as they entered, they could hear someone breathing. John froze as Lyndquist went for the light switch. A moment later the room was illuminated to reveal Meyers apparently sound asleep in his bunk, undressed, oblivious to their presence.

"That's him. That's definitely the man," John whispered. "He must have run back here and jumped into bed—"

"Meyers, wake up!" Lyndquist ordered, suspicious the man was faking. "Get up, damn it—"

Meyers slowly rolled on his back and grimaced in the light. "What's up?" he asked in a raspy voice.

"Where have you been the last hour?"

"Where have I been? Right here, asleep. I've got an

early shift tomorrow." He sat up in his cot. "What's this all about, anyway?"

"He's lying," John interrupted, although troubled by the man's milder manner and normal voice.

Meyers looked at him. "I don't know what you're trying to pull here, mister, but I've been right here in my bed all night and you can—"

"What about the broken lock on your door?" Lyndquist said.

"I don't know anything about it. Did somebody try to break in? Is something missing?"

"No, nothing's missing, but someone who at least looks very much like you went out to the hub and threatened some of the researchers—"

"And you think I did it? That's crazy. Why should I? I haven't been out there in months."

As the man was denying the accusation, John went to his closet and brought back a torn uniform. "It's the right sleeve, just like the professor said." John showed the evidence to Lyndquist.

It was indisputable. He had to be the one, in spite of his persistent denials. Until an investigation could be conducted, Lyndquist ordered Meyers confined to his quarters.

The crewman continued vehemently to deny the charges, but as the commander, John and the security guard went out and closed the door behind them, Meyers' eyes glazed over, his face emptied of expression and he turned toward the porthole, through which he stared and kept on staring—as if transfixed.

XXXIII

By the thirtieth day of gestation Cortney was back to her usual self, cheerful and enthusiastic about the pregnancy. There was a healthy glow to her cheeks and in thinking back they decided it was probably the rest more than the intravenous fluids that had done it. She'd gotten herself into a vicious cycle, worn out, not sleeping, each day compounding the problem. Now that was all behind her and she was looking forward to the remaining eight months.

She soon resumed her daily exercises and was eating double portions of food. Her lost weight rapidly returned, and they could put her on standardized regimen to maintain a daily two ounce gain, measured daily on mass scales whose measurements had to be mathematically converted.

Meyers remained confined to his room and vehement about his innocence, but Lyndquist wasn't taking any chances, at least not until Dr. Stull had finished his assessment. But after a week of interviewing, the neuropsychiatrist's conclusions were ambiguous and confusing—something that was tearing him apart. He needed a clear diagnosis for a definite course of therapy, but nothing seemed to bear out.

He could determine that Meyers had some deep-seated religious feelings, but he usually kept them to himself. Being away from his family and friends had been upsetting, but not more than for any other crewman, and he didn't seem to know much at all about Olmschied's work. He wasn't even sure what level they were on. He denied being bothered in any way by Cortney's pregnancy, and other than a few jokes with other crewmembers hadn't given it much thought.

Before submitting his final report, Stull also went into

Meyers' history, but here too the clues to his aberrant behavior were non-existent. He was from a suburban home and one of four children, he'd been a good student in highschool, average in college, a reliable hard worker since joining the aerospace program. His friends considered him to be shy and none of them could remember any instances of erratic behavior or sudden flareups.

His sexual interests were also normal. He had a girl friend waiting for him that he planned to marry once his tour of duty was over. Repeatedly, Stull asked him how he felt about sex between unmarried partners, such as John and Cortney, about homosexuality, bestiality, and every time his response was plain indifference... "to each his own," summed it up. He didn't have any philosophical thoughts about Olmschied's work, no religious associations, and despite the seemingly incontrovertible evidence, he maintained his innocence. If it hadn't been for the three witnesses and the torn uniform, Stull would have sworn that they had the wrong person. He still couldn't make a diagnosis. He even tried hypnosis, hoping to bring out some hint of a split personality, but the man's psyche remained solidly intact. Finally, needing *some* label, he concluded that the crewman had to be a *well-guarded* schizophrenic, or merely walking in his sleep. Neither diagnosis fitted him at all well.

When John heard the sleepwalking diagnosis, he rejected it immediately... given those two choices, Meyers had to be a schizophrenic. During his training he'd seen a few patients sleepwalking and not one could have been that violent without waking themselves up first. Usually their eyes were closed and his had been wide open. Whatever, his actions certainly seemed purposeful, and dangerous. John and Dr. Olmschied insisted that Lyndquist send him back home.

The next shuttle flight was due in three days. When Meyers was told about their plans, he strongly objected, saying that they were sentencing him without a trial and he'd bring a civil suit against them the minute he got a chance to hire a lawyer.

Here he'd threatened John and Cortney with pain and death one night and now *he* was talking about a lawsuit. And, astonishingly sincere about it ... or so it seemed. Well, lawsuit or no, Lyndquist wanted to take no chances on a potential Jekyll and Hyde.

When the day came for Meyers' departure, however, things didn't go as smoothly as they customarily did. Usually the shuttle flights were as routine as bus trips between cities on earth. Not this time. Before take-off the shuttle flight had all sorts of mechanical problems and two substitute rocket boosters had to be brought in. Twenty-four hours later the shuttle finally blasted off, but as it passed through the ionosphere the computer cross check system failed—the fifty cross checks a minute were down to one, and being unsure of their computers, the pilots had to turn around.

Two days later a second shuttle flight was attempted with a different vehicle and this time all power was lost at the same latitude. All systems were dead, including auxilliary back-up, and after hours of hunting for the cause the ship was forced to glide back to earth on manual controls.

Both ships checked out normal once back at Mission Control. No explanation could be found for the breakdowns, but pending a more in-depth investigation the shuttles were temporarily grounded. After all, three times was still out.

XXXIV

BY THE sixth week of gestation Cortney's body began showing many of the external signs associated with pregnancy. Her usually small breasts had become more prominent and were filled with the glandular tissues that would ultimately produce milk. Her pink nipples had taken on a maternally tan hue and there was a slight but distinct bulge in her lower abdomen.

Meanwhile the holograph showed the fetus steadily taking on a human appearance. Legs and arms were followed by hands and feet. The head looked like a child's, but when compared to the rest of its body it was outsized, slightly grotesque. The eyes were set widely apart, open and without eyelids and there were minuscule nubbins for ears. From crown to rump it measured thirty millimeters (one and a half inches) and deep within this tiny person was a heart now beating regularly. The baby's own blood began perfusing its body.

Throughout each day and night John kept watch over Cortney, helping when she didn't feel well and encouraging her to exercise when she did. He made sure that she napped at least two hours each day, ate everything they brought her and slept eight hours a night. . . .

It was a day toward the end of the seventh week. Dr. Olmschied entered Cortney's room, a smile on his face. He seemed very pleased with himself as he approached her bed. "All right, boy or girl, lady . . . speak up or forever hold your—"

"Can you *tell* yet? Is it really time already?" Cortney asked excitedly. John got up and quickly came across the room.

"You didn't answer me. Boy or girl?"

"Come on," John said, "enough games. Which is it . . . ?"

"A boy," Olmschied said proudly, almost as though it

were his. He pulled the holograph photo from his pocket to document.

"Are you really sure?" Cortney asked, looking at it.

"Ninety-nine percent. I guess that small item *could* be a loop in the umbilical cord, but I doubt it."

The three of them were delighted. It was going to be Adam after all.

XXXV

ON EARTH, the shuttle flights continued to have trouble. Repeated attempts to reach the Space Lab from other take-off sites met with the same mechanical failures. One attempt was even tried from its sister satellite, Space Lab IV, but it too failed, and General Boelling became concerned about the lives of the three thousand men and women on board.

The shuttle flights were the most sophisticated rockets available, each with three main rockets that carried 500,000 pounds of thrust and two solid rocket boosters with an additional five million pounds. The larger rockets couldn't travel the distance needed and those with less thrust couldn't carry passengers. In the past, an alternative means of space travel wasn't necessary. Now, it obviously was, but new construction would take years.

Not only did Mission Control need a new way to reach the Lab, but scientists were also given the chore of finding out why this was happening. An electrical barrier of this sort was unheard of and although there were plenty of theories, that's all they were. So far, there weren't any facts to be analyzed or any measurements to be made. It was an invisible shield. Everyone knew it was there, they just couldn't see it.

Scientists at M.I.T. attributed the problem to an unnoticed sunspot or solar storm, but others argued that if this were so all satellites would be similarly affected, and they weren't. A team at Cornell thought it had to be a magnetic cloud that would eventually pass . . . when, they couldn't say. When it finally came down to it, the least probable seemed the most logical—an alien vehicle, vehicles, of some sort with remarkable powers were responsible. The similarity between Gregor's crypts' malfunction and the rocket-engine malfunctions were too obvious to overlook. Someone, some thing apparently didn't want anyone coming to or going from the Space Lab, and with that in mind Boelling warned Lyndquist to be on the lookout for another visit.

Cortney's pregnancy progressed into its eleventh and twelfth week. All of her physical symptoms were gone and the holograph indicated that the baby's maturation was exactly on schedule; no adverse effects could be found.

Her problem was boredom. Even after Olmschied lifted her restrictions, she still felt imprisoned. True, the hub was five levels high, but instead of being confined to a single room she was now confined to a building—an unnatural building. The walls were rounded, the ceilings too low, the air stuffy and, of course, the pervasive lack of gravity. Planting her feet on the ground and merely going for a walk was something she'd always taken for granted. Now it was a swim.

At night John slept beside her, but during the daytime he often took to wandering along the outer rim, using a variety of excuses to get away. He, too, was restless—he missed the surgery and the pressures of his work; he had trouble coping with nothing to do. His conversation turned lackluster . . . oh, he continued to try, but spending nearly twenty-four hours a day with one person—even one you were very fond of—was a bit much and especially hard on the supply of sparkling conversation. . . .

Drs. Baumeister and Olmschied kept to their established routines—Baumeister making his daily rounds, logging his conferences, Olmschied keeping out of the limelight, assessing every measurable aspect of Cortney's pregnancy. If they were going to have any trouble, he wanted to know of it at the earliest moment. She had already passed the tenth week, the time during which an abortion could easily be done, and now with each passing day, the safety of doing the surgery was rapidly diminished.

At times Olmschied would set aside his testtubes and spend time with Cortney, talking about old times or some new journal articles, but as the days wore on they more often stared at each other in uncomfortable silence.

To break the monotony Cortney would occasionally climb up into the bubble and sit with Kreuger. The blanket of jewels was his home, and he gladly shared it with her. With Kreuger her narrator-guide, they took in the astonishing sweep of the heavens, from Jupiter's twelve moons and the frozen rings around Saturn to the gigantic Horsehead Nebula of Orion and the exploding Crab Nebula of Taurus. He led her across the skies to double and triple stars, to glittering giants that seemed to be racing away as if the universe were expanding, and to others that were closing in as if it were collapsing. They visited quasars, white dwarfs, and empty spaces where black holes were thought to exist. He pointed out to her the newly discovered planets in Sagittarius and the distant tail of Halley's comet. . . .

At the other end of the space lab satellite, crewman Meyers was also staring out into space. His eyes were focused, riveted, on Alpha Centauri; whenever he was interrupted he became violent. Dr. Stull had to bring a security guard into the room with him whenever he came for his interviews, which had become name-calling sessions. Meyers blamed the psychiatrist and "his kind" for instituting a religion on earth that was more dangerous than any of the favorite "so-called religious sects" of the past. He guaranteed the doctor that the world was now finished.

He said it solemnly, almost calmly, like a judgment.

His abrupt change in tone as he said it gave Dr. Stull some very unscientific goosebumps.

XXXVI

IT WAS the middle of her thirteenth week. Cortney had just left Kreuger's perch.

Captain Thompson put in an emergency call to Lyndquist. "We've picked up something coming our way again, sir. Radar places it about five hundred thousand miles out, but it's traveling almost as fast as our beam."

"One of those so-called UFO's? Well, we were alerted to expect something—"

"But the image is larger than before. I've already notified General Boelling."

Instead of going straight to the command post Lyndquist headed for the hub area. He could just as easily direct things from out there, and this time he wanted to track the vehicle's approach with the telescope. He considered sounding the alarm, decided not to . . . if it were like its predecessors it too would stop at ten thousand miles out, circle for a while and leave. He devoutly hoped so, because the failure of the shuttle flights had still not been solved. If anything happened, it was damned unlikely they could count on help from earth.

When he did arrive at the bubble, he found Kreuger's eyes trained on the same quadrant that the meteor had come from, but instead of a glowing orangish-red light as before, this one was changing . . . first yellow, then green, then blue.

"Keep a low profile. Don't antagonize them." Boelling's voice resounded from their speaker, and was followed by an identical echo.

Lyndquist tried focusing in on the approaching light, but the glare bothered him. Each time it hit yellow, the brightness nearly blinded him.

"Damn it, it's like looking directly into the sun," he said, and backed away.

"Shall I sound the alarm this time?" Kreuger asked.

"No...not yet."

At fifty thousand miles, the thing was orange and by ten thousand, it was blood-red and still rushing toward them.

"It's not stopping, that son of a bitch is coming straight for us—" Lyndquist hit the alarm himself, hoping that he hadn't waited too long.

As the shrill sound filled the ship's corridors, the vehicle continued toward them.

"What are you doing? You're down our throats," Lyndquist called into the radio transmitter.

"What are you doing? You're down our throats," came an identical response.

"My God, why don't they talk to us?"

"My God, why don't they talk to us?"

At fifty miles out, it suddenly slowed. Every porthole in the Space Lab was filled with its blood-red color. Radio communications with Boelling turned to static, and the air was filled with a high-pitched, screeching sound.

"Shall I fire?" Kreuger hollered, taking hold of the laser and aiming at the center of the light.

Boelling had told them to avoid a confrontation if at all possible, but the glowing object was still coming at them as if it intended to ram them. Unable to communicate with it, Lyndquist decided he had no choice. He ordered Kreuger to fire. The crewman took steady aim, pressed the trigger button. Nothing happened. Suddenly all of its power was gone, just as with the shuttle flights and crypts before.

Its size was enormous, at least ten times the Space Lab's, its sound deafening. Lyndquist and Kreuger started backing down the ladder toward the nearest cubicle. Everything around them was blood-red.

At fifty feet, the thing stopped and hovered over the satellite like a vulture waiting for the kill. The two men reached the cubicle but found its doors sealed shut. Lyndquist pounded on the outside, ordering someone to let them in, but his voice didn't carry. Inside were John and Cortney, terrified by the awful sound they were hearing. All that Lyndquist and Kreuger could do now was cup their ears and curl up for safety.

What seemed an eternity was a matter of seconds. As the thing closed in, an armlike projection extended from its underside, the hand opened, and a conical object dropped onto the bubble, careening off the rounded surface and settling a few meters away. Then, the arm-like projection slowly withdrew into the bright light and the whole thing began to back away.

It took several minutes for Lyndquist to regain his thoughts. He'd never had a migraine before, but felt pretty sure that the pain he was feeling was at least comparable—his eyes were blurred, his ears rang incessantly, and his guts were awash in nausea. Overhead he could now make out Boelling's voice: "Space Lab Five, Space Lab Five, come in. This is Mission Control. Can you read me?" Every word vibrated in his head, and hurt.

"Yes, I can read you, I'll get back . . ." Lyndquist finally blurted out, and started back up into the bubble with Kreuger right behind. In the distance, they could see the "visitor" disappearing in a rainbow of whirling lights.

"I'm sure glad they didn't decide to stay for dinner," Kreuger said weakly as he started checking over his equipment. The power supply to the laser was back, now that it was too late.

Lyndquist nodded, but before he could resume contact with Boelling, his eyes caught sight of the conical object.

"What the hell is that?" His immediate concern was that it belonged to the Space Lab, but on a quick inspection of the exterior hull, nothing seemed damaged.

"Looks like they brought us a present."

"Or a bomb of some sort," Lyndquist said.

Hesitant to sound an all clear yet, Lyndquist dispatched select teams to check for leaks. The master panel in the command post indicated everything was secure, but he wanted to double check. Meanwhile he headed toward the maintenance dock. Someone had to go outside to check the exterior hull and he didn't want anyone going near that object until he personally had a chance to inspect it.

Maintenance kept three vehicles on standby, each a one-man device shaped like a pyramid with four separate windows, two sets of mechanical arms and a variety of propulsion rockets that could move it in to different directions at the same time. After putting on a pressurized space suit, Lyndquist took the closest ship.

He began his surveillance along the outer rim, the most critical area; no signs of damage. The sun's side gleamed and the earth side was dim, but nowhere was there the slightest dent. Moving along the darker side, he slowly made his way toward the foreign object, checking for radiation all the while, but the levels never exceeded normal background.

"Can you tell what it is yet?" Thompson broke the silence. Both he and Boelling were watching Lyndquist on a televised screen.

"I think it's metallic...at least it looks like a metal alloy...they're some hexagonal boxes fused together, maybe some type of measuring equipment and...this may sound crazy, but there's a sort of crumpled umbrella at one end...and there's some broken antennae...."

"Be careful," Boelling said from Mission Control, trying to get a closer image of the object, but Kreuger's bubble was in the way.

Lyndquist continued a circular approach, slowly and carefully moving up on it. He had the strange feeling that he'd seen this thing before. He couldn't place it, but somewhere in his past he'd come across something damn similar....

Once he was within a few feet, he stopped the pyramid and, carefully nudging the object with the mechanical arm, braced himself for an explosion. There was none, it merely bobbed like a cork on water.

"At least it doesn't explode," he said. "I'm bringing it in. Make sure we have isolation equipment ready."

Catching the two ends in the mechanical grips, he slowly backed up toward the dock. It took him almost a half hour, and each time he looked back he got the same eerie feeling... he'd definitely seen this thing before... a photograph, a diagram, a dream...?

A team dressed in protective suits was waiting to receive it, and once the dock area was repressurized they converged on the object. Lyndquist, still in his suit, stepped out of the craft.

The object seemed charred, and as they scraped away some of the black soot one of the men said, "Hey, it's one of *ours*."

"How do you know?" Lyndquist asked, coming over to look more closely.

The man pointed to an inscription, and although it was worn the words were distinctly "Pioneer X." The same satellite he'd seen on the cover of one of his old school textbooks.

"I'll be damned," was all that Lyndquist, or any of them, could say. The Pioneer X satellite had been launched into space twenty years ago, and the last he'd heard, it had been lost. What he especially remembered about it, though, was a gold plaque—it had made headlines in 1971—and he immediately began searching for it.

He found it bent in half along one of the broken antennae. Using a screwdriver he quickly pried it away and, after flattening it, found the message pretty much as he recalled it: the sun with its nine planets, the pulsar diagram, the binary equivalents and the images of a nude man and woman. It was all there, with one difference— someone, something, had put a hole through the woman's abdomen.

XXXVII

THE MOMENT the all clear was sounded Dr. Olmschied unlocked his door and quickly headed for the hub. All the time he was confined in the emergency cubicle, visions of the previous meteor collision and the mysterious lights of the unexplained vehicle took over his thoughts. He could see John and Cortney being sucked out into empty space, helpless, gasping for nonexistent air in an endless vacuum of dying a fiery death. And he blamed Baumeister . . . after all, they wouldn't have even been here if it wasn't for his calculated blackmail.

As he hurried through the gathering crowds in the corridor, he eavesdropped on conversations among crew members, but no one seemed to know what had happened. Everyone had felt the vibration and been deafened by the accompanying sound, but there were no evident casualties. He hoped that that was the case in the hub as well.

When he got to the South elevator he quickly strapped himself in and pushed the button for the central core. A moment later a voice reminded him to buckle up and he was on his way. The lights, the pressure, the oxygen all worked. Everything seemed in order.

As the doors parted he was standing, poised to rush out. He barely got three paces before meeting John, carrying Cortney in his arms. "My God, is she all right?"

"Some cramps. Whatever that was, it gave her a real scare," John said. Cortney tried to smile, gave up. Her face was very pale.

Olmschied helped him get her back to her bunk, where they strapped her in, and John went for some sedation. Worried about a possible miscarriage, he wanted to calm her down soon as possible.

"Any bleeding?" Olmschied asked.

"No." Cortney shook her head, reached out to hold the

professor's hand. "No, this baby will hold on. He's a tough one."

Olmschied squeezed her hand.

John returned with the syringe in hand, wiped her shoulder with alcohol and injected its contents. The medication worked almost instantly, and once they were certain she was calm and resting, they began reconnoitering the nearby laboratories for damages. Each room they checked was in perfect order. It was as if nothing had happened. When Olmschied tried raising Lyndquist, he was told the commander was busy and an explanation would be coming soon. He began to get angry. Someone had better tell him what was going on.... Remembering that Kreuger's lookout station was right above them, he started toward the ladder, but was scarcely halfway up when he heard his name and Baumeister's being paged to report to Maintenance immediately.

Peculiar, hardly the place where he wanted to be, but the voice sounded urgent. He reversed directions, rechecked Cortney and headed for the North elevator. He couldn't remember where Maintenance was, but since he'd never seen it he assumed it was on the opposite side of the outer rim—the north end.

The elevator let him off in the crews' quarters and a few meters away he found a sign for Maintenance. A bit further he found the entrance. Baumeister and Lyndquist were inside.

"What's this all about?"

"I need both your opinions. We had another visitor, but this time they came closer and actually dropped off an old space probe of ours—Pioneer Ten. I'd like you to take a look."

"I don't know about these things, Commander," Olmschied told him as he followed him toward the twisted wreck.

"You don't need to." As they came to the gold plaque, Lyndquist explained the purpose of the Pioneer mission and what the message was for. He then pointed out the two figures with the hole in the woman.

"That wasn't there when it was sent up. I already checked with Mission Control."

"It must have been hit by some tiny meteor," Baumeister quickly said. "How long was it out in space?"

"Twenty years—"

"Ample time for damages of this sort."

"Maybe," Lyndquist said as Olmschied now bent down for a closer look, "but the hole's too perfect, too smooth. It's not like any meteor hole I've seen before. The edges should have buckled from the impact or melted from the heat. It looks more like someone *drilled* it."

"That's absurd. Besides, what would the *purpose* be?"

"I don't know. That's why I asked you and Dr. Olmschied here."

Olmschied stood back up and wiped his glasses. "You think it has something to do with Cortney and the baby?"

Lyndquist shrugged. "Could be—"

"I don't believe it," the surgeon cut in, obviously against anything that might threaten going on with their experiment. "It could mean almost anything, and *I'm* sure it means there's just been some sort of random accident . . . no need making mountains out of molehills."

Olmschied disagreed. "I doubt that someone . . . something would bring this satellite back to us from millions of miles away and drop it on our doorstep just for the random hell of it. As much as I hate to admit it, it appears as if they *are* trying to tell us something . . . something none of us wants to hear—"

"But suppose it isn't a threat at all—suppose it means just the opposite?"

"Such as?"

"Well . . . maybe it's a warning about the baby's life in utero. They saw what we were doing, knew about some potential danger and this is their way of warning us. If they wanted to . . . well, to kill Cortney or the baby, they could have done it by now. They've demonstrated they could have killed everyone on this ship. Personally I don't think that hole's much grounds to assume anything, least of all a threat. It definitely would be a mistake to jump to any conclusions—"

"You don't really think," Olmschied said impatiently, "that they came all this way to warn us about some potential pregnancy complication by putting a hole in this figure's stomach?"

"Could be, you don't know—"

"That's idiotic. I think they're trying to tell us something, and I think we had better listen."

"Olmschied, you've wanted this experiment to end all along. You opposed me from the first, wanted an abortion when it was only morning sickness, and now this—"

"Yes, I was opposed to it in the beginning, and for good reasons, but now that it's started I want to see it through . . . remember, though, thanks to you we've got a crazy man locked in his room, no shuttle flights and a pregnancy of my colleague that might not only fail but endanger her—"

"Gentlemen," Lyndquist interrupted, "this isn't getting us anywhere. If I could ship this thing back to Houston, I would, but without the shuttles we have to solve it here. I need your help to find a rational approach, so please let's cool off."

The only useful suggestion was Olmschied's that they check the equipment inside for other similar holes. Should there be any, it might put the death threat to rest.

Lyndquist agreed. For the next two hours the Pioneer X satellite was carefully dismantled. Every nut, bolt, transistor was laid out on a plastic sheet and closely studied, but *nowhere* could they find the slightest mark of any kind.

XXXVIII

HEADING BACK toward the command post, Lyndquist forced himself to look hard and close at the situation. If this were truly a threat against Cortney's pregnancy, what would happen if they didn't go along? And what was going along? An abortion? Was his ship and crew in jeopardy, or Cortney alone? Or was it even a threat? There was still the possibility that the hole was some freak accident, though he doubted it. Why else would they have brought the satellite back?

When he finally resumed contact with Boelling, the general was equally undecided. Neither wanted to commit himself without more information. But with the presently defunct shuttle system there was no way to move the satellite back to earth, where it could be properly evaluated.

The next best thing was to set up a video relay system from the Maintenance Department on the Space Lab to Mission Control. Every part of the Pioneer X satellite was photographed, macroscopically and microscopically. Data from the remnants of its memory banks were radioed to ground computers and series of chemical tests were set up to hunt out any clues about the life forms they might be dealing with.

Dr. Olmschied had made his way back to the central core, and tried to play down what he'd seen. "It was just one of those damn flying saucers that came too close this time," he said as he crossed the room and headed toward his workbench. He wanted to wait and discuss the finding with John later, but Cortney could see the concern written on his face and confronted him.

"There's more to it than that, isn't there?"

Olmschied looked over, debating on how to phrase what he'd seen. John and Cortney waited impatiently for

171

his answer. "A plaque..." But his voice was too subdued for them to hear. He repeated himself..."a plaque...the...uh...UFO brought back an old satellite with a plaque on it—"

"One of the Pioneers?" John interrupted.

"Yes. How do you know that?"

"It has to be a Pioneer if it had a plaque on it...I think I can even tell you what was on it if you give me a minute—"

"Never mind," Olmschied stopped him. "It was just a bunch of mathematical equations—"

"And a body of a man and woman, right?"

"...Yes."

"That's it?" Cortney said, confused. "They almost destroyed the Lab to bring back an old satellite?"

"There's a bit more to it than that," Olmschied reluctantly added, realizing that she'd have to know sooner or later. "The plaque wasn't the same as when it was originally sent up. This time it had a hole in it." He hesitated. "A hole in the woman's abdomen...." As the words came out, he immediately regretted them. Cortney turned pale as her hands reflexively went to her abdomen.

"They're not going to hurt this baby," she said, looking first to Olmschied and then John. "I won't let them. They *can't*."

John moved closer and put his arms around her. "Nothing's going to happen," he whispered, hoping to convince her more than he had himself. "There's got to be another explanation—" He turned to Olmschied, inviting his agreement, for the moment at least.

"It could have been a small meteor," Olmschied offered, "or maybe a defect in the alloy. Or both. The commander's setting up to run some tests."

"But if the hole's an accident, why would they bother bringing it back in the first place? And why to us?"

Olmschied couldn't answer her.

XXXIX

THE ANALYTICAL work at Mission Control proceeded slowly. Videotape relays were converted into twenty thousand single photographs, studied and then compared to diagrams and photos taken from their archives. Each microscopic shot was meticulously examined for scales, hairs, stains, fingerprints, smudges or any other unusual markings. Nothing was detected. It almost appeared as though the inner machinery had been purposefully wiped clean. Under normal circumstance there should have been at least a few human prints....

When the scientists turned their attention to the IPP, the imaging photo polarimeter, they discovered that its calcite prism had been fractured, recently and probably on purpose. The same was true of the two detection telescopes. Both lenses were cracked by a direct blow, lenses that could have provided information about the unknowns.

General Boelling was particularly interested in the satellite's last days, but the memory banks reacted as though a black veil had suddenly descended over them. All radiation bombardment had ceased, the charged-particle composition experiment had stopped and the plasma analyzer, which looked backward at the sun and studied wind particles, measured zero. The only information they got was that the Pioneer probe had not died a natural death—something they already knew.

The days waiting for word from Houston turned into weeks, and still no decision. The mounds of collected data were passed on to Dr. Leigh and the Space Commission Board, then to the Joint Chiefs of Staff, and finally to the White House. The hole might or might not be a threat, no one could say for certain. The President would not recommend an abortion on such flimsy evidence—nor would any of his advisors...and of course some questioned whether he or they had the right in any case, especially if the mother objected. Instead he decided that Cortney be removed from the Space Lab and brought back to earth as soon as the shuttle flights resumed.

Meanwhile Lyndquist was gearing up to fight off this thing if it returned. Extra men were assigned to keep watch, the laser guns were shifted to a better-shielded auxilliary power unit. Lyndquist's annoyance at the delay in getting a definitive response from Houston was offset some by the fact that at least the unknown vehicle had disappeared as mysteriously as it had come. Each day they expected to see it again, and each day the skies were clear.

The first twenty-four hours of waiting for an answer were probably the hardest on Cortney. There was no place to hide, and in her mind everything hinged on her pregnancy. The notion of having an abortion was abhorrent to her, and yet if she refused, might she not be responsible for others dying. It was an awful dilemma, especially now that she felt the baby moving. To her he was as much alive inside her as if he were already born. If it came to it, she knew she could at least argue effectively with her own people, but she didn't know what to expect from *them*... who knew, maybe, they'd send across some sort of invisible rays, like those that knocked out Gregor's lab, or teratogenic viruses that might cause her to abort spontaneously. Not knowing what to expect was the worst.

She began to feel nearly paranoid about what she ate, where she went and what she did. Food tasting the slightest bit off to her was instantly discarded, specks in her water were carefully screened out. While the others slept at night she stood as if on guard with her eyes to the porthole, watching for the return of the changing lights. She didn't have the slightest notion what she would do if she actually saw them, but was determined that at least they wouldn't catch her sleeping.

By the end of the fourth week of waiting she finally began to relax a bit. Fatigue was part of it, but she'd also rationalized that they wouldn't have left her alone this long if they were actually a threat. Seeing that no harm had come to her or her baby so far, she concluded that Olmschied and the others had to be wrong. She wanted them to be, desperately, so they were.

By her fifth month, most of her worries were gone. Occasionally she would think about the plaque—how could she not?—and occasionally a strange noise would wake her in the middle of the night, but John was always there to check it out and each time he found nothing more than an apologetic crewman passing by.

In reaching her fifth month, Cortney had also gone beyond the so-called point of no return... the child was legally alive, fully functional although still premature if born, and too dangerous to Cortney to abort. If he were to be delivered now, there was a good chance that he could survive, and if an abortion were performed it could be thought of by many as physiological murder... not to mention the extreme danger to Cortney. Her dilemma resolved itself. Now, for sure, she was going to have her baby.

Meanwhile, the gentle nudges inside her abdomen became field goal attempts. He'd kick her through the navel one minute and across the flank on the next. The harder they were, however, the better she felt. This way he had to be healthy, a fact confirmed on the holograph.

It was a day six weeks after the plaque arrived. John came into the laboratory with a huge present gift-wrapped in computer paper. Cortney ripped through the mathematical columns, opened the carton, and inside found a wooden cradle John had made from a shipping crate he'd sanded and stained.

"It's beautiful," she said delightedly, rocking it back and forth as if the baby were already inside it. It was the first time she'd dared to give any thought to preparing for the baby's actual birth.

By the sixth month the effects of prolonged weightlessness were starting to show. Her legs were weakening, and although she faithfully kept to the prescribed exercise program and counted her calories, it became more difficult each day to move about. John was beginning to feel it too, but at least he could go to the outer rim whenever he wanted and shake the feeling. As the days passed, though, it would take him longer and longer to get his legs back in shape.

He was afraid that the change for Cortney might be crippling. . . .

XL

THE SPACE LAB remained isolated in outer space, and the stress of being stranded there was beginning to tell on the nerves of crew members. Tempers ran short everywhere, fights a daily occurrence. The Space Lab satellite itself was functioning well. Food remained plentiful, although almost entirely vegetarian now, water continued to be pure, oxygen levels remained stable, and as long as the sun continued to shine the satellite's power system could last indefinitely. Still, the thought that they just might not get home again was a damned nervous-making one.

At Mission Control scientists had managed to uncover the type of magnetic interference used on their shuttles and were busy working on a new resistant prototype. The basic design and instrumentation were the same, but like the lasers, it had additional shielding and a fourth rocket to carry the heavier load. If all went well, the first test flight was expected to be ready in six months, long before any serious shortages could occur. Everyone was anticipating success.

When Lyndquist announced the news over the intercome system, Dr. Olmschied was the only one who didn't seem relieved. He'd been following a slow upward trend in Cortney's blood pressure as well as a trace appearance of protein in her urine. The changes were still subtle (pressure going from 120 over 70 to 130 over 80), but to him they suggested the pregnancy might be headed toward toxemia, a complication that often caused high blood pressure, convulsions and spontaneous abortions in its usual form and could be fatal to both mother and child.

True, at this point in her course it was still only conjecture that she'd get worse. Such symptoms occurred in many pregnant women who never developed toxemia. But that was earth . . . here, he didn't know what to expect.

And when he checked the Lab's pharmacy he discovered it didn't stock the customary medications to treat it. Anticonvulsants, antiarrhythmics, and antibiotics—but not prostaglandins. It was an oversight on their part—and his—when they decided to go ahead with the experiment, and now with the shuttle flights grounded he could only hope that Cortney's pressure didn't continue to climb. . . .

Cortney hadn't actually felt any of the ill effects. Fatigue persisted, but other than the nuisance of being tired she felt confident she'd make the nine months. Which was only eight more weeks! On the holograph the baby was near term-size, fully developed and extremely active. Each day when Olmschied checked her, she watched the sonar image with immense pleasure. There, curled up inside her, was a new person, about to make his debut, and sure to become the finest baby ever born, on earth or in heaven.

In the outer rim Meyers was also beginning to get more active. He'd been kept in confinement since the shuttle flights were grounded, allowed out once a day with a guard, and now was demanding that they set him loose.

Although the psychiatrist had not been able to fix a diagnosis, Lyndquist had heard Meyers' screams during the night. He sounded like an animal in pain, and yet when they opened the door he'd be sitting there, apparently as rational as anyone else. Lyndquist was taking no chances with this Jekyll and Hyde. Nor was he able to dismiss from his mind that Meyers' behavior, which defied the psychiatrist's ability to diagnose, was somehow directed, influenced by an influence outside his satellite . . . and beyond the ken of all of them.

XLI

IT WAS a night during the beginning of the eighth month. Cortney was up visiting Kreuger. John was asleep in the laboratory. Meyers started screaming again, but this time he could be heard halfway around the outer rim. Lyndquist's refusal to set him loose had apparently set off a series of nightmares, and soon he began throwing his body against the locked door. The guard on the other side had been instructed not to enter his room alone, but when he heard a particularly loud crash, a whimper and then silence, he figured that Meyers had really hurt himself. He unlocked the door and went inside. Meyers was waiting. He grabbed the guard by the throat and tossed him against the wall, where he fell unconscious. Then he locked the door behind him, headed toward the kitchen, where he stole a carving knife. His eyes were dilated as he entered the South elevator.

Kreuger's astronomy lesson was just ending. These days Cortney tired much sooner, and instead of her usual hour or more she was ready to leave after thirty minutes. Tomorrow they would take in the Andromeda Galaxy, and she took a book with her to read up on it. Thanking Kreuger and apologizing for the brief visit, she started down the ladder.

Meyers exiting the elevator at the hub didn't know Cortney was still on the ladder, coming down. He slipped quietly into the laboratory ahead of her and started toward the bed that he remembered her being in. It was too dark to make out faces. The moment he reached the body that was wrapped in the covers, he jammed his knife into its midsection. John screamed out in pain, momentarily unaware of what had happened. Standing above him was Meyers, screaming like a man possessed . . . "no babies, no babies . . . you should have done what they told you . . . you should have listened to them. . . ."

As Cortney entered the room she heard the man's screams. She switched on the light, and saw him standing over John's blood-stained blanket. She started to run to John, and as she did Meyers started toward her, his knife raised above his head.

At that moment the injured guard had managed to reach the intercom in Meyers' room and notify Lyndquist, whose immediate thought was the laboratory and Cortney. He ran toward the elevator shaft, afraid that he might be too late. Coming in from the opposite direction were three armed security men, who were told to shoot Meyers if necessary. . . .

Cortney was slowly backing up into the corridor, trying to close the door. Meyers was instantly there. She struggled ineffectually to hold it, but the door gave way and Meyers was in the corridor with her, still raving "no babies, no babies," and still holding a knife red with John's blood.

Above them Kreuger heard a scream and immediately recognized Cortney's voice. He dove through the passageway, his small body easily fitting through the portal, and within a second was on their level behind Meyers. He saw that Cortney was cornered. Pushing off, arms spread like a bird, Kreuger knocked Meyers aside with his fist and called to Cortney to get out of there, but Meyers quickly took a swipe at Kreuger and then blocked her passage. Kreuger dove again, throwing his body against the man's side, then flying off. Meyers stumbled, but not enough to give Cortney room to get away.

Kreuger's tactics, though, had killed enough time for Lyndquist to make it there, and as the commander entered the corridor he ordered Meyers to leave Cortney alone. . . .

Again Meyers angrily intoned his "no babies" and then, looking first to Lyndquist, then back to Cortney, "God wills me to do this—"

"God doesn't will anyone to kill another human being," Lyndquist said, trying to buy some time.

Kreuger didn't wait. Spotting a metal basin just inside

the laboratory door, he grabbed it and loosed himself at Meyers again, knocking the knife free with the first pass and catching him across the forehead on the rebound. The knife darted across the room, barely missing Lyndquist, as the crewman returned to club Meyers along the temple, the bridge of the nose and down the back of his neck until he was unconscious.

"You've got to help John," Cortney said, terrified. "He's been hurt badly...." There were tears in her eyes.

As the two men hurried inside they found the room filled with free floating globules of blood. John was trying to climb from his bed but, too weak, slumped forward.

XLII

By the time Drs. Baumeister and McLaughlin arrived at the hub John had slipped into shock. His skin was cold, clammy; his respirations rapid and shallow. Baumeister called for six units of artificial blood and put a pressure dressing over the wound. He'd have to get him to surgery, but the only operating room was the delivery room. It had most of the equipment he'd need, and with McLaughlin's assistance he hoped that they could make it through. At least the dog procedure, although a different operation, would help him know what to expect.

The stored blood arrived in moments, but as the intravenous lines began to flow, John's blood pressure still didn't register.

"That son of a bitch must have hit an artery," Baumeister blurted out as he tried starting a third IV to increase the flow and told Olmschied to take Cortney out of the room.

McLaughlin now hurried into the delivery room, scrubbed and began setting up for an abdominal exploration. It had been a while since he'd assisted, but a surgical tray was already wrapped in case Cortney had an emergency, the IV bottles were lined up on the shelves. He summoned a medic who'd worked with him and was also a qualified nurse anesthetist. The man arrived in a couple of minutes, and they notifed Baumeister that they were ready.

Baumeister, though, was hesitant to move John, whose blood pressure was only faintly discernible after the first three units. Still, if he could stabilize him first, the risks of surgery could be minimized. His early gut reaction had been to rush John into the O.R. and stop the bleeding, experience told him to hold back. He ordered three more units of blood and started running preliminary studies on John's blood count and electrolytes.

Outside the doorway, Cortney was beside herself. "If I hadn't been so stubborn, if I hadn't kept the baby this would never have happened—"

"You're not responsible for what a crazy man does," Dr. Olmschied said, feeling more than a little guilty himself. "If you have to blame someone, blame me, not yourself or the baby...."

"Oh, God...if he doesn't make it...."

"He'll *make* it. Baumeister may not be my favorite human being, but he may just be the world's best surgeon."

Cortney nodded, trying to take some comfort in his assurance.

After the fifth and sixth unit had run in John's color improved. His extremities had gone from a purplish color to pink again, and he was moving. His blood pressure had progressed to the low normal range and his respirations slowed. Baumeister immediately added the seventh and eighth units to the empty lines. Whatever was bleeding inside, at least the loss was slower than the infusions.

John continued to improve, and thirty minutes after they'd begun the intravenous lines he began to waken. At first his speech was garbled, but he slowly regained his senses and remembered what had happened.

"How bad is it?" he asked Baumeister.

"Pretty bad. He hit something important. Think you're up to surgery today?"

John hesitated a moment, then said emphatically, "No, I'm not."

"Or course you are. McLaughlin's standing by, all we need to do is move you next door—"

"Not until I see Cortney."

"Cortney's fine, John, you'll see her afterward...."

"I'm not going until you bring her in here."

Nodding, Baumeister went to the doorway and called Cortney into the room. "He wants to see you, but stay only a moment. Now that he's stable, I want to get him to surgery before we start going the other way."

As Cortney entered the room, she was smiling and crying at the same time. She went to his side and held his hand.

"At least you and the baby are okay," John said, trying to lift up, but was too weak. "At least I'm glad I was there and not you—"

"I wish none of us had been there."

"I've decided not to have surgery."

"You what?"

"Well, at least not until you marry me . . . Cortney, the boy's got to have a father, a legal father . . . I mean just in case I don't—"

"That's ridiculous," Baumeister interrupted. "You'll be fine . . . and we'll have a big ceremony afterwards—"

"No, *now*." John's voice was still weak, and an occasional cough caused severe abdominal pains.

"That's blackmail, you know," Cortney said quietly as her fingertips glided back through his hair. "The least you could do is propose."

"Okay, will you marry me. . . ."

"Yes," she said without hesitation, realizing that marriage was what she'd wanted too and had been too stuck in past miseries to admit. But this was an awfully drastic way to come to such realization.

"All right, for God's sake, somebody get Lyndquist back up here and tell him to bring his book."

Five minutes later the commander had pronounced them man and wife.

Baumeister was already in his scrub suit and John was then hurried into the O.R. His blood pressure was beginning to slip again and his color fading as he was anesthetized.

Baumeister made his incision, a long vertical cut that would give them sufficient room to assess the damage.

"If he doesn't get an infection from that knife, he'll be awfully lucky," McLaughlin said as he struggled to suction the massive amount of blood loose in John's abdomen.

Baumeister agreed.

Although the external wound was barely over an inch in length, Meyers' knife blade had penetrated the large intestine, lacerated the gall bladder and liver and severed a major abdominal artery. Each was a major injury and together presented a bleak prognosis.

Stopping the blood loss took priority over repair. Baumeister immediately clamped both ends of the severed artery. That had accounted for nearly half the blood loss, but it seemed they'd have to come back to remove a short section of small bowel that might turn gangrenous. Next he looped three deep stitches across the liver laceration. They were tenuous in the soft organ, but they held. Now, the gall bladder would have to come out. It was impossible to repair it, and since it wasn't a vital organ he quickly proceeded to make the appropriate incisions. Finally he had to contend with the large bowel, where the cut was leaking fecal material into the abdominal cavity and adding to the threat of peritonitis (compounding those from spilled gall bladder bile and the dirty knife). He made a temporary colostomy and repaired the wound.

The surgery took five hours to complete and required six more units of blood. Throughout, John's blood pressure teetered near shock levels, but as they closed both men were more worried about the threat of infection than the extent of the injuries.

"Beautiful job," McLaughlin told Baumeister as they left the OR and took off their gloves. "Best I've ever seen."

Baumeister thanked him, adding that he was more at home working above the diaphragm and could live without too many cases like this. Physically, he was exhausted. Operating on a friend had something to do with that. . . .

Meanwhile, as Meyers was regaining consciousness in a security cell, the outsider's vehicle was hovering a thousand meters beyond the portholes of the Lab. It had come while they were operating, and throughout, echoed conversations between Baumeister and McLaughlin. When the surgeons were done, it stayed. All of its lights were out, and it remained as a dark shadow against the distant starlight. And silent.

XLIII

DURING THE next seventy-two hours John remained in serious condition, and there were several times that they thought they would lose him. Somehow, though, he always managed to rally back at the last moment. His white count, key index of severity of infection, was six times normal; his temperatures hovered around 104 but often crept up to 106. Each time that they thought they were making some headway, his temperature would spike upward again and he'd lapse into a coma. But Baumeister nor McLaughlin were about to give up.

Baumeister and McLaughlin alternated twelve hour shifts, and by the third day both were exhausted. John's complications taxed all their knowledge. Almost every hour his vital signs changed and they had to readjust the intravenous fluids, or his respirations became labored and they'd have to change the oxygen. Every antipyretic on board was tried, including an ice mattress, and still the fevers persisted. Three different antibiotics were administered around the clock, and still his bloodstream was cluttered with microorganisms. If the fevers didn't break soon, they doubted he could hold on much longer.

Cortney kept in touch via the intercom system. Because of the infection, Baumeister wouldn't allow her to visit, but whenever John was lucid he'd put them in contact, making it appear that John was doing better than his doctors knew.

Outside, the darkened vehicle continued its hovering vigil, not moving, not changing. It had clearly keyed on Cortney, echoing every sound she made, including her breathing at night and the baby's heart tones. Each time that Lyndquist radioed Mission Control, he could hear the incessant, pulsing lub-dub sound in the background.

Each time he tried making contact with it . . . them . . . the only response was lub-dub, lub-dub, lub-dub . . . one hundred and sixty times a minute.

XLIV

ITS CONTINUED presence alarmed Dr. Leigh sufficiently so that after the third day he called a combined meeting between the Space Commission Board and the Joint Chiefs of Staff in Washington. If matters came to a head, the scientist wanted the two groups to coordinate.

Among those present: General Alexander Younger of the Army, General Lester Waters of the Air Force, Admiral Arnold Lewis from the Navy, Secretary of Defense Fischer, Dr. Freyberg, Dr. Smith, and Dr. Leigh, who chaired the meeting.

Dr. Leigh began: "As all of you know, we now have ourselves a tenacious visitor." He dimmed the lights with a remote switch and began a series of slides. "It comes in a variety of spinning lights, though as you can see it's totally black at the moment. Our measurements make it some five miles across, bigger than the earlier visitors; it does not seem to need gravity unless it's rotating internally; its speed is variable, but our estimates put it close to the speed of light: and it seems to come from the area of Alpha Centuri." Leigh changed to a few close-ups that showed a darkened, smooth surface. "There's no armament as we know it, but needless to say, no one knows what its capabilities are. Hostile? ... perhaps, but if it's interested in that baby, the pregnancy has less than two months to go—"

"And if we'd *stopped* that ridiculous pregnancy a long time ago we very likely wouldn't be in this mess," General Waters angrily put in as the lights came on. Outspoken, he'd objected to the President's decision to wait and watch.

"Well, it's too late now," Dr. Smith said in a milder tone. "We need to let ... them know that we have peaceful intentions—"

"Oh hell, we've been trying to do that all along. Why don't you send them another satellite with a cute plaque on it. If the Pioneer hadn't carried a road map, we wouldn't be in this predicament—"

"There was no way to have known at the time," Dr. Freyberg said, stung by the General's accusation.

"Well there should have been some foresight—"

"Gentlemen," Dr. Leigh broke in, "there's no point in starting off with an argument. The past can't be changed and we have a *problem* before us that needs solving."

The Army's General Younger took it up. "The one thing we can't do is give in. I think we should push this thing until it either makes its move or makes us understand what it wants, why it wants it, and what it will do if we don't go along. If it can fly here from God knows where, over God knows how many millions of miles, it certainly ought to be able to communicate intelligibly. It's time we found out what kind of enemies, if any, we do have in space—"

"You want to gamble with the lives of three thousand men and women just to see what it'll do?" Dr. Smith said.

"If necessary, yes. It wouldn't be the first time we had to use people as decoys to test the enemy, and you know it...in some countries it's standard operating procedure—"

"This isn't war," Dr. Leigh told him.

"And this isn't some ordinary enemy nation," Dr. Smith quickly put in.

"True," General Younger said, "and we don't know what they have in mind...to them this might be the beginning of a confrontation...maybe we should strike first...."

The expected differences between the two groups were apparent from the outset—the scientists more inclined to wait and work to improve communication; the generals, angered and frustrated by the persistent harassment, considering a means of retaliation. On one issue only were they in agreement...the abortion of an eight-month-old fetus was intolerable.

Alternatives were hashed over and rehashed—if they attacked the space lab, if we attacked the visitor, if other vehicles came and this time turned on earth en masse, not just selectively as apparently up to now, and finally if they did nothing. To end the stalemate, Dr. Leigh recommended they send a lone emissary out to "the damned thing to express in person *our* desire for peace . . . not that we give up, but to see if we can make some meaningful contact and see how they react. . . ."

None of the generals liked the idea but they went along. Secretary of Defense Fischer took the recommendation back to the President that evening.

Two hours later the order to send an emissary was radioed to Lyndquist.

XLV

THE CONTACT flight was scheduled for 0900 the following day. The vehicle selected was the only thing they had—a repair module, the same as Lyndquist had used to retrieve the Pioneer satellite. Mission Control felt its obviously benign appearance would help assure its safety. Lyndquist had his reservations. In fact, he had reservations about the whole plan. To him it was potential suicide. Not only did the small pyramid lack armaments, it could never achieve sufficient acceleration to return home if attacked. Feeling as he did, it was impossible to ask for a volunteer. He accepted the assignment from himself.

In preparation his command post began radioing its intentions four hours in advance. "We're sending a manned vehicle out on a peaceful mission" was repeated over the airwaves at twenty minute intervals until the last half hour, when they stepped it up to every five minutes.

Lyndquist and his men also attached a mile-long nylon cord to one of the mechanical arms. Remembering the mechanical failures of the previous shuttle flights, he hoped that they could reel him back if his engines failed. The Lab end was attached to a powerful winch, while the cord itself was a five-ton test line. It was cumbersome, but seemed the best chance he had.

When the time came to board, Lyndquist had the feeling—kept strictly to himself—that he wouldn't make it back . . . it was similar to the feeling he'd had when he boarded the Apollo flight years before, except this time he felt as though he were holding a loaded revolver to his head. If they hadn't responded by radio by now, he doubted that they'd be exactly greeting him with open arms . . . that is, if they had arms. He thought how he'd once made fun of "creatures from outer space," laughed at the science-fiction movies and books. Well, he wasn't laughing now....

As he fastened the last snaps on his space suit he stared out at the men around him and made up a smile, then climbed inside the module. Moments later he had jettisoned himself from the Lab. Behind on his desk lay a letter to his wife and children.

"Give him plenty of rope," Captain Thompson instructed the men at the winch, then headed for the command post.

The radio broadcast shifted to every minute..."We're sending a manned vehicle out on a peaceful mission...."

In contrast to other broadcasts, however, the echos had abruptly ceased. When Lyndquist reached the three hundred meter mark, the black disc took on an amber light. He promptly slowed, but it didn't move. Beneath him, his engines functioned smoothly, his gauges were functioning, and most of all he was still breathing properly. It was obvious that they knew he was coming but so far had not interfered. He continued.

At around a hundred meters the disc suddenly changed to a red, a blood-red.

"Commander, I'd say you ought to come back, they don't seem to want you out there," Thompson was saying.

"Not yet," though he was tempted. Instead, though, he pulled his sun visor down to cut down the glare and pushed forward.

At five hundred meters the disc went black again, blocking out most of the sky, seemingly lifeless.

"What the hell does that mean?" Thompson was saying.

"Maybe it's hiding," Lyndquist said. Nobody laughed. "Make sure that winch is still working."

The minute-to-minute repetitions of the peaceful-intent message continued as Lyndquist drew near. At a hundred meters out it seemed the exterior was...furlike? Yes, by God, in fact almost hairy, and with huge projectiles lying on top of each other...Maybe he was having some sort of hallucination, a wierd disorientation, but damned if this didn't seem to be a ship at all . . . if it didn't seem to be, well, some sort of enormous living organism. . . . He shook his head, trying to clear it of such thoughts. My God, this thing was five miles across. . . .

Lyndquist groped along the circular base for several minutes hunting for some entrance, a place to land, but it was all the same . . . *hairy* surface. As he climbed over the edge he saw a huge furry dome in its center with a necklace of metallic balls around its base, and on closer inspection each of these seemed more like metallic saucers hitchhiking on this monstrosity. Or perhaps controlling it. . . .

"If I didn't know better, I'd think this thing was *alive*," Lyndquist said to Thompson, almost apologetically, and then repeated it to himself. The main body looked like no spaceship he'd ever seen . . . no portholes, no entrances, only miles of these hairy projections.

Now his engines started failing. A moment later the interior of the module began losing pressure. He was being drawn closer to the dome. He tried starting up the auxiliary unit but it too was dead. At fifty meters from the dome two enormous yellow protuberances . . . *eyes* . . . opened and stared into his module.

"Get me out of here," Lyndquist yelled. "This thing *is* alive, for God's sake."

As the winch began drawing the slack line Lyndquist's module drifted closer, he could see a pincher arm grasping the base of his craft and another coming from the opposite direction. . . . "Can't you get that damn winch going, this thing's got arms, and it's got hold of me—"

"The line's taut, it won't give."

"Then shoot the damn thing—"

Kreuger heard the order, confirmed it with Thompson and aimed his laser dead center. An instant later the beam burned into the underbelly. The entire being turned red and an enormous roar sounded. It threw Lyndquist's

crumpled module across space and started toward the
Lab.

"Hit the alarm," Thompson ordered, but the word
came too late. As the winch pulled free and ripped
through the outer wall, taking three men along, the
outrageous thing took a firm grip along the outer rim and
began shaking them as a child would a rattle. Everyone,
everything was flung through the air, bouncing off walls
and ceilings. People were screaming in the corridors,
unable to grab a holdfast to steady themselves. Cracked
heads, broken arms . . . hardly anyone escaped injury.

And as the ship's rotation scheme was lost, and its
power began to fade, this thing kept shaking them.
Endlessly, mercilessly.

XLVI

THE BUFFETING lasted a full ten minutes, and when it was finally over the thing returned to its thousand meter perch and watched, as though it had, for the moment at least, vented its anger. Even from the distance, though, its yellow eyes were clearly visible.

Inside the Space Lab all was shambles. With gravity control gone, the ship and its occupants hung helplessly in space. Cold stellar air was beginning to cool the interior, lights were out, oxygen levels were falling and water from ruptured tanks was seeping into living quarters. The only system still holding was pressure control, and on it depended their survival.

The moment the ship settled, Captain Thompson struggled to his feet, not believing what had happened. Both his shoulders were badly contused and an oozing laceration was above his left eye. Outside their porthole he could see Lyndquist's module floating away with its long nylon tail and three dead crewmen nearby, but his first priority had to be the ship's turbines. There was no way to know if the commander had survived, but without electrical power everyone's life would soon be critically threatened.

He went to the intercom, found both audio and visual components knocked out. Switching to emergency auxiliary power, a battery system for the command post only, he was just able to pick up audio with the chief engineer, whose report was bad. They'd been fighting an oil fire, two turbines were irreparably damaged and the third needed parts he wasn't sure they had. If they were lucky, it would take his men another hour. If not, it could be days. Or never.

Thompson told him he'd have to do it in an hour. The

ship's reserves wouldn't last much longer. Now he shifted his attention to organizing teams to check for leaks and help the injured. The critically injured could be moved to the infirmary, the others less serious would have to wait in the emergency cubicles.

Last, and first among his own priorities, he sent a pilot out after Lyndquist's craft. The man had a fractured femur, but it was stabilized with a splint and he was more than willing. Thompson had to pick among the least badly injured.

In the hub, the laboratories were totally dark. Loose equipment floated everywhere. Fortunately, Cortney had been resting in her bunk when the attack came, and she'd been able to ride it out. Dr. Olmschied was not so lucky. Seated at his desk, he'd been catapulted to the ceiling, where he'd been instantly knocked unconscious. Cortney was now calling out his name in the darkness, but there was no answer. By holding her own breath, though, she could hear his breathing—a stertorous sound—somewhere close by. She got out of her bunk and started inching along the wall toward the sound. Without lights it was extremely difficult to keep herself oriented, but having been isolated in this room for months she knew every crevice, every shelf, every angle by heart.

She finally located him lying face down in a corner. He was limp, unconscious. She did her best to check his hands and feet for fractures, decided, so far as she could tell, that there were none. But when she moved his head she felt warm blood from a deep laceration in his scalp. Pressure was the only thing she could think of. She tore a piece of cloth from her dress and covered the gaping wound with her hand. And then she waited...two minutes, three, five minutes...no one came. She'd have to do more.

Realizing that the intercom was dead, she tucked a blanket around him and went out into the corridor. Normally during the daytime there were a dozen or more technicians working. When she called out now, the only

response were a few distant moans. To get help she'd have
to get to the outer rim. She'd been warned not to make
such a change without help, but knew she had no choice.

Out in the corridor she found the going more difficult.
Not only was the enclosed passageway darker, but at each
step she bumped into some object suspended in
mind-air—a carton, a bottle, test-tubes, rubber tubing,
lab coats...they'd hit, then bounce away like corks on
water. Once, when she blindly tripped over a metal box
floating a foot off the ground, she immediately stood up
into a serpentine maize of electrical wiring and had to
fight her way free.

It took her fifteen minutes to travel forty paces, and
when she finally reached the elevators none was working.
She tried calling out again, the only reply were distant
moans. She banged on the doors until her hands hurt; no
one came. She stood here, indecisive. Dr. Olmschied
could be dying, and here she was stranded in the darkness.
And why? It had to be that ship, or whatever it
was...and what if it came again? She started back toward
her own room, a hand brushed up against her face. It
lingered a moment, then its icy fingers moved across her
cheek, up to her forehead. Panicked, she looked up and
saw a dead man's face inches away. His face was frozen in
a grimace, almost smiling. His eyes were wide open as he
returned her stare, his arms hung down as if trying to
embrace her. She began to scream, no sound came out.

She had fainted.

At the opposite end of the ship John was struggling to
free himself...one of his legs had been trapped when his
bed slammed shut and he'd been pinned there ever since.
Nearby, Dr. McLaughlin was slumped against the wall,
dazed by a blow to his head.

Still working on the leg, John thought he could hear
the trickle of water. At first it seemed to be coming from
deep within the walls, but soon a small bubble appeared,
followed by a second and a third, each coalescing into a

larger whole . . . the room was on its way to being flooded.

"Chet, damnit! Wake up and open that door!" But Dr. McLaughlin was too confused to understand.

John levered his arms against the edge of the bed and pulled with every last bit of strength, but there was little of it. He tried arching his back against the wall to pry the bed loose. No luck. The spring mechanism was jammed. Within minutes the water bubble was half the size of the room, and still growing.

"Somebody, help!" he called out, but the closed door swallowed his words. "Damnit, Chet, wake up and get us out of here—"

The physician tried to focus on what John was saying, but the words wouldn't register. His expression remained blank.

"Damnit, *try* to hear me. Go to the door and let the water out."

McLaughlin didn't move.

John felt panicked. The water was already seeping into his mattress. He began clawing away at the stuffing to lessen the grip. The foam rubber flew away like goose down, handful after handful until there was a little give to his leg. Seeing some results, he worked even harder. Each time he bent forward the incision in his abdominal wall ached viciously but he forced the pain out of his mind. He felt like throwing up. The fever was making him sweat and chill at the same time. He kept digging—digging and calling out to a man who, despite being a foot away, couldn't hear a damn word he was saying. Digging, and praying, that Cortney was all right.

Slowly the leg slipped through, but by then he was exhausted. He could barely pull himself out, but someone had to get through the water and open the door. He doubted he could do it. He tried explaining the situation to McLaughlin again, but the best he got was the physician repeating his words, words that had no meaning for him.

Finally, every alternative exhausted, he somehow

managed enough strength to give McLaughlin a good
shove. He floundered forward, fell into the bubble face
first. For an instant he seemed to float inside it without
moving, then suddenly the cold temperature brought him
to. Arms flailing, he fought his way out . . . and mostly by
reflex opened the door.

"Thank God, I thought you'd never wake up," John
told him.

McLaughlin looked back, dazed, still unsure of what
had happened.

Outside, the second repair module was chasing
Lyndquist's craft, but the pilot would have to hurry to
catch up . . . the momentum from the cosmic toss was
carrying Lyndquist further away every minute, and there
was a limit to how far the rescue vehicle could go. If
exceeded, both modules would end up stranded.

Still, if he were to gain on Lyndquist, the pilot had to
keep the module at maximum speed. In the distance the
first craft looked like a twisted wad of tin foil, hardly
unrecognizable as a repair module. Still attached to its
base was the original tow line and at its far end was the
winch with part of the floorboard attached. The three
bodies that had gone out with it were slowly scattering to
the stars. None had been wearing space suits.

As the second ship's fuel tank was approaching the
halfway mark, the pilot had to make a decision. He had
already reached the winch, but there wasn't enough time
to make it to the module. He extended the mechanical
arms and latched onto a ridge, braced himself for the
breaking maneuver and once secure, started pulling
Lyndquist back toward home. Almost an hour had
elapsed—the maximal amount of oxygen that Lyndquist's space suit could have stocked.

High above them, the yellow-eyed being was watching
the attempted rescue. Far below was the crew of the Space
Lab. One clearly wouldn't help and the other couldn't.

As the two modules were nearing the Lab, the lights

inside suddenly came on. The third turbine had started working, and with it the satellite began slowly to revolve again. There were cheers for the lights, and for the recovery, but as yet, no one knew if the commander was alive.

Once the winch was on board, a team quickly reeled the attached module inside, then immediately set down to cutting a window at the end where they expected Lyndquist's head to be. They found the back of his neck instead and quickly had to flip the module over and start again. The hour limit had already been exceeded. A few more seconds lost seemed critical.

The crewman working the laser beam cut the metal frame like a surgeon, swift and precise. A metal square was lifted away, and inside they found Lyndquist semicomatose from lack of oxygen. He was still breathing, though, and there was a pulse in his neck, but his color was ash gray, his skin ice cold.

Captain Thompson stood by when they finally raised the commander's body from the metal shell. Prewarmed, one hundred percent oxygen was administered by mask and an electric blanket was piled on top. No one knew where McLaughlin was, but the treatment of astrohypothermia was part of basic training.

It took several minutes for Lyndquist's color to return to normal, and as he slowly woke he was shivering beneath the covers. He could barely talk, but he managed to ask Thompson for a report on the damages.

"They're pretty bad, are you sure you want to know?"

Lyndquist shook his head yes.

"There're two holes in the external hull, one in maintenance where your winch broke through, another off storage depot B. Two turbines are out and we're barely making it on the third. Almost all of the plants in Hydroponics have been uprooted and the area looks like an old-fashioned tornado went through it. The vegetable farms are half destroyed. Radar and communications are still out but we should have them back before long. Two aquariums are wipe outs. Half the ship's been affected—"

"Any deaths?"

"Five that we know of. The three who went out with you, one from the storage depot and Meyers. One of the broken aquariums flooded his cell. He couldn't escape."

XLVII

IT TOOK the crew two days working round the clock to restore the satellite back to some semblance of normalcy. The lone turbine continued to hold them, but the electricity it generated had to be carefully rationed. Most of the ship's corridor's were darkened, three of the four elevators were shut down, temperatures kept at a barely tolerable 58 degrees—that is, everywhere except in the Hydroponics Section, where the plants depended on the maintenance of a special environment.

Worst was the number of crew members injured, and dead. Five hundred were seriously injured, seventeen had died. During those first twenty-four hours, Drs. McLaughlin and Baumeister... Baumeister too had received several bad contusions... worked steadily setting bones and swing lacerations, and by the time they were done the ship's infirmary was badly depleted of bandages, plaster, artificial blood and analgesics.

Throughout the crisis period, though, John's condition continued to improve. Both doctors would have predicted a worsening after his exhausting struggle, but instead his fevers dissipated and his strength gradually returned. The only explanation was that the antibiotics had either cumulatively taken hold or there was a sudden surge of IV fluid during the attack.

In the hub, all was now nearly restored to its pre-assault status.

Cortney, found lying next to the South elevator, was revived with smelling salts.

Dr. Olmschied took longer to come around, having incurred a concussion and a deep scalp laceration that required seventeen stitches. But the moment McLaughlin had finished tying his last knot, the old professor was back on his feet and attending to Cortney. The upset had adversely affected her blood pressure, and the readings now were ranging around 150 over 90. If she continued to stay that high, the threat of toxemia was very close.

When communications with Mission Control were re-established, General Boelling and Dr. Leigh were stunned by Lyndquist's report. Neither had expected such a violent attack, and both were apologetic for having provoked it.

"It's too late for apologies," Lyndquist told them sharply. "That *thing*, animal, whatever it is, is still hanging around out there. We can't take another beating—"

"Animal?" Leigh asked.

"Well, it's not vegetable or mineral. It's *alive*. Believe me. There's a cluster of metallic beads, each about the size of a planetarium dome, around its neck. My guess is that they're how it's controlled, or maybe our visitors live *inside* them, like an overgrown horse and rider—"

"And you believe it still wants you to give up the baby?" General Boelling was asking.

"Who knows *what* it wants now . . . it's been silent ever since, but I don't have much doubt that that's what it seemed to want before. . . ."

"Well, I think you should hold out, especially since you don't know what it wants," Dr. Leigh said. "We don't need another death. . . ."

"So you suggest that we sit here and just wait, or ask polite-like that it tell us what it wants? Which it hasn't done up to now . . . I don't think that we can afford to sit here much longer. Maybe the damn thing can't talk, not our language, anyway . . . anyone consider that possibility? It's got a bad temper, I'll vouch for that. I don't think we can make it another six months until your shuttle flights get up here to bring us back."

"I've already ordered them to be sped up—"

"Can you have them here by tomorrow?"

"I can in three months—"

"Too late."

"Look, Commander, I know it's relatively easy for us here, and you're the ones on the line, so to speak, but we've got to try to stay cool and try to formulate a new approach—"

"You formulate...I've got a funeral to go to, seventeen, in fact. Seventeen eulogies wrapped up in one. Send the families your formulations."

Boelling tried to hold him, but the screen was dead.

As dead as the feeling inside Lyndquist as he realized that this time it was going to have to be his decision alone...and that...that—much as he hated the idea—an abortion would now have to be considered.

After the seventeen caskets were set adrift in space he returned to the quiet of his quarters to consider the alternatives. During the last six months of waiting there had only been one attack, and perhaps it had been provoked by the laser. Since then, the *thing* had remained placid, watching. Maybe it was waiting for the child to be born, and if it survived, make its move then, or maybe he and others were completely misinterpreting its actions. He just didn't know, and he hated the thought of ordering the death of an unborn child on speculation. He hated it, and he also doubted that he could go through with it, especially now that it was so near term.

As he undressed and put on a robe, he found an envelope stuffed in the pocket. He immediately ripped it open and found a scribbled note inside.

Commander:
   It's us or that baby. If you don't make the right decision soon, we'll have to do it for you....

XLVIII

THAT EVENING Olmschied worked late in the laboratory running an assay on placental blood flow. The test was difficult and it took him hours to complete it. When he finally analyzed the nuclear markers in Cortney's bloodstream, the evidence was clear that the movement of nutrients to the baby was failing. If it continued, the child, and possibly Cortney's life, would be seriously in danger. Olmschied immediately went to Lyndquist's room and woke him up.

"We have to get a shuttle flight up here right now," he began as he came inside. "Cortney's going into toxemia, I'm afraid. We need some prostaglandins—"

"You need prosta...whatever they are, *I* need a few things myself and can't have them. Professor, I couldn't get you an aspirin from earth if your life depended on it—"

"That's just it, her life probably *does* depend on it. At least the baby's does. Untreated, she may lose him."

Lyndquist stared at the professor for a minute and thought of the threatening note. The loss of the baby could be the answer to that problem...it was one he wouldn't have to order, one he actually didn't have control over....

"You've got to do something," Olmschied went on, "this is too dangerous a thing to let go on—"

"What do you expect me to do? I can't carry her on my back down to Mission Control." Lyndquist saw the look on the professor's face and apologized. "We're all stuck here, Dr. Olmschied. That thing out there could come at us again any minute, and we're a sitting duck. I don't know, professor, maybe this is nature's way, maybe this baby just wasn't meant to be—"

"Nonsense," Olmschied said angrily, "you'd be cold in your grave by now if medicine had felt the same about appendicitis or pneumonia. If we went along with so-called nature's way, I doubt most of your crew would still be alive or you'd even have been born. Nature's way stopped being man's way centuries ago, and if this thing, as you call it, wants to reverse that, we've got to fight it—"

"Maybe not reverse...maybe keep it in our own backyard...hell, I don't know, professor, but I *do* know I still can't help you...isn't there anything else you can do?"

"Operate and take our chances with a premature baby. I doubt that he'd survive, though. At this early stage there's a ninety percent chance that he'll develop a respiratory distress syndrome...his lungs aren't mature yet, and we have nothing here to treat it if he does."

"How much time do you need to improve his chances?"

"Two weeks, maybe three. It's hard to say, every case is its own, but I don't think Cortney can make it. It may reach a point where we have to choose between losing the baby or losing them both."

Lyndquist, feeling the professor's anguish, felt less than proud of his earlier cop-out thoughts about the baby. Sure, he wanted to survive, and he had a command responsibility, but there were ways and ways....

Whoever signed that damned note would have to go through him before they could get to Cortney and her child.

XLIX

JOHN'S FEVER was now gone and he was moved back to the laboratory to convalesce near Cortney. Still weak and pale, he couldn't accept being away any longer, especially now with the possibility of toxemia. She'd want him to be there when it came time to make a decision, and besides, it was his child too. . . . So far, Cortney wasn't aware of the on-rushing crisis.

When he arrived, though, she seemed to sense something was wrong, that he wasn't as excited about the baby as he'd been earlier. Maybe, she thought, it was on account of his prolonged illness, but the professor wasn't himself either. The last two days he'd been quieter than usual . . . more serious, almost depressed. Finally she spoke up. "You two look like your best friend died. Everyone's so quiet, it's almost spooky."

"Everything's fine," John said, but his voice was less than convincing.

"Then why the foot-long face? Let me assure you, gentlemen, I feel fine. A little fatter than I'm used to, but that's okay. And so is Adam. He lets me know he's uncomfortable and can't wait to get out. He's not shy, I guarantee you."

As John affectionately laid his hand across her stomach, the baby kicked as if to confirm what she'd said. "Another one of those and he may break out on his own," he said, forcing a smile.

"Just like I told you. There's nothing to worry about."

John, of course, knew otherwise. He'd seen toxemia as an intern. He watched as Olmschied took her pressure again and saw that it registered 152 over 98.

"What's it today?" she asked.

"A little high, nothing to get alarmed about," Olmschied said, trying for nonchalance, but Baumeister happened in the room just then, looked over his shoulder and said without thinking, "152 over 98. Still creeping up but—"

John angrily glared at him as Cortney also looked concerned. Hypertension was something she knew wasn't good for an expectant mother.

"I was about to say, but no need to worry."

"How's that?" Olmschied said, thinking once again that this would never have happened if they'd completed the monkey studies first to learn the dangers. "Cortney understands . . . it's a little higher than I like to see it. . . ." With the bad news out in the open, no need to dissemble any further.

"I've been looking at the formulary in the pharmacy and they've got a medication that we used to give for this years ago. Used it before operations. I must have ordered it without remembering. Maybe it's there for some other reason. It doesn't matter, though. I can't see any reason why we can't use it."

"Magnesium?" John guessed.

"Right. Good old elemental archaic magnesium. It used to do the job pretty well."

Baumeister then immediately left for the pharmacy, but when he arrived he found the doors locked and a sign outside saying "be back in five minutes." He waited, not wanting to budge until he had the vials safely in hand.

Five minutes became twenty before the pharmacist's assistant returned and casually asked what he wanted.

"Magnesium sulfate."

"Don't think we have it." The crewman sounded confused. The pharmacist was still out and he hadn't heard of the medication.

"I know you do. I already checked the formulary. It's an old-fashioned treatment for toxemia."

The assistant's attitude changed to immediate interest. "Toxemia?"

"Yes, Cortney's got a little problem with her blood pressure, but we'll have that straightened out quickly. Can't let it affect the baby. . . ."

The man pointed to the pharmacy's directory, then left

claiming an urgent errand. His faintly agitated behavior didn't strike Baumeister, a man not noted for his awareness of the feelings or reactions of other people. He went about his search not really aware that the assistant had left.

Opposite the drug's trade name he found the shelf number and then proceeded back into the rows of glassed cabinets, half of which had been fractured during the assault. Everything was back in place, though, and he found the medication sitting on a top shelf under the letter M—a small carton of twelve vials, more than enough. He started to leave some behind, but thought better of it. No need to take any chances.

He started back out . . . and found himself confronting five crewmen with helmets and clubs.

"What's *this* all about?" Baumeister demanded, backing off.

No one spoke. The five directed him back into the recesses of the pharmacy, where two of them grabbed his arms and a third dumped the vials out on a countertop and proceeded to break each one.

Pinned against the wall, Baumeister, shocked, told them they'd kill the baby, that he needed the medicine badly.

"And it'll kill us if we don't," one of them said, and, half-apologizing, proceeded to cold-cock the surgeon with his club.

Baumeister lay on the floor for several minutes before the pharmacy assistant returned and, pretending upset, immediately called Lyndquist. When the commander got there, Baumeister had regained consciousness, rubbing his head, but told them he'd no idea about the identity of the men who'd attacked him. Broken vials were strewn across the floor among tiny pools of the needed medication. No mystery about the seriousness of that.

Guards were now stationed outside the laboratory doors around the clock. Whenever any of the doctors traveled to the outer rim they were accompanied by security guards, and all medications that they might need were transferred to Olmschied's workbench. Lyndquist also had his officers search the ship for weapons, including even potentially dangerous kitchen utensils, which were confiscated and the door to the machine shop locked.

In a sense the ship had become a prison ward. While they waited to see if Cortney's pregnancy terminated itself, there were guards with guns and precise rules and regulations. Any behavior out of the ordinary, any meetings, any loitering, was immediately brought to Lyndquist's attention.

Convinced now that Lyndquist was determined to protect the child regardless, they began to strike back ... at first with relatively important placards, then soon after, Lyndquist and Thompson began receiving letters threatening their lives, warning them to watch everything they ate, not to sleep at night, not to trust anyone and that soon everybody on the ship would be against this "Jonah."

Lyndquist was angry, but he didn't let it carry him away. He went to the ship's intercom and asked for cooler heads. He explained how seriously ill Cortney was and how the child very likely wouldn't survive in any case, but they couldn't just end a pregnancy that was nine tenths to completion. He told them new shuttle flights were due soon and that while he understood their fears, none of it justified murder.

Cortney was listening to the broadcast, horrified at what she was hearing. Having been isolated in the hub, she had no idea that the crew had turned against her and was now threatening violence. Earlier, when Baumeister had returned empty-handed, he'd told her that he'd been mistaken about the formulary but that they had other means to treat her. Now, according to what she heard from Lyndquist, she was expected to lose the baby in a matter of days, the baby she felt kick inside her. None of this seemed real. The infant was as good as being outside her now, healthy and bawling, alive and well. Oh, God. . . .

Thirty minutes after Lyndquist's speech, he got his answer. The electrical wiring to the command post was cut, and one of the partially damaged aquariums totally smashed. A note left behind read: "We won't need the food. There'll be plenty back home once the baby's gone."

As a team was repairing the severed wires, a new problem presented itself . . . outside the portholes there now appeared a dozen of the beings, all with their changing light schemes, totally encircling the Space Lab satellite, inside of which the unknown baby's heart beat began echoing once again.

Not one, but a dozen echoes to each beat.

L

Lyndquist refused to be intimidated, by those outside or inside. He ordered Kreuger to stand by with the laser, and to use it "if those things come any closer."

He was sure they could hear him, after all they'd heard everything else, which was fine with him... he wanted them to know he was not about to give in to them, or any of their surrogates on-board... He moved to the porthole to check out any change. The twelve darkened monsters were still hovering around them, but at least none had advanced closer.

But if Lyndquist's bravado... and he recognized it for what it was... helped morale some, it did nothing for Cortney. The combined effects of stress and toxemia threatened her pregnancy. The level of protein in her urine had quadrupled overnight, her pressure had increased to 180 over 110 and she'd become extremely irritable.

To keep her from seizing, Baumeister initiated anticonvulsants and began an anti-hypertensive medication for her blood pressure. It was hardly the one he'd pick under normal circumstances, but the situation was hardly normal and there was only one blood-pressure medication on the ship. For the first few hours she seemed to respond, but then the baby's heart rate began to slow. First 140, then 130, and then 120. The only option left was to operate, take their chances on prematurity. To leave the baby in utera now would guarantee its death.

As far as Baumeister was concerned Cortney had no choice, and asked John to explain in detail to her. She might be a skilled and learned scientist, but she was also very much a woman.

It was the hardest thing he'd ever been asked to do. He loved her, knew how much she wanted this child, how she'd fought to keep it, how much *he* wanted it too....

"Adam's quiet;" she said.

He leaned over and kissed her. "He's also having some problems—"

"I know, you don't have to tell me. It's time, isn't it?" She looked directly at him, her face terribly serious.

He nodded. "Yes . . . it's time, Cortney." There was no need now to go into details. She understood without them.

As Baumeister set up the operating room, Olmschied worked on an incubator. Increased levels of oxygen would be added through an inlet valve if necessary, but if the baby had hyaline membrane disease from being premature it would hardly suffice. Originally when they'd ordered their equipment, no one anticipated that they wouldn't be able to get a sick baby back to earth. At the time Olmschied's only worry was that the whole experiment was premature . . . not that the shuttles would be knocked out. . . .

As Dr. McLaughlin gave her a pre-operative injection, John stood beside her. Their hands were clasped together.

"He's going to make it," Cortney whispered. "You'll see. I ought to know how tough this guy is. . . ."

John nodded, but knew otherwise. The child was only thirty-five weeks. If the slightest thing went wrong and persisted, they were ill-equipped to handle it.

A last minute check on Adam's heart rate showed it to have fallen to 90. The operation had become an emergency. McLaughlin rolled Cortney into the operating room. As soon as she was under anesthesia Baumeister made a midline incision, dissected down to the abdominal cavity and exposed the bulbous uterus inside. The pulse had lowered to 80. Changing scalpels, he quickly opened the womb, grabbed the tiny baby by his legs and hoisted him out as McLaughlin clamped the umbilical cord. His color was bluish, and Baumeister gave him a swat on the behind. No response. He hit him again. Nothing.

"Get me an ambu bag," he sanpped, and quickly suctioned the amniotic fluid from the baby's mouth.

A moment later he was pumping air into the child's lungs. Slowly the baby started to move its limbs. It tried to cry, but was too weak to make a sound.

"Don't cry, just breathe," McLaughlin heard himself say as he pinched the feet to stimulate it. "Just *breathe*."

For fifteen minutes they pumped oxygen into his weak lungs until he was able to take over for himself, then he was moved into the warmth of the incubator and the two doctors turned their attention to Cortney's incision.

The entire procedure had taken just under an hour. As Baumeister left the operating room he proudly announced that mother and child were doing well. "The baby's a little puny, is all...."

John and the professor were ecstatic, but Commander Lyndquist, who'd been waiting with them, had to be concerned about what would happen next from the ones outside. He immediately went to the porthole and saw the twelve of them moving inward. An instant later, Kreuger was on the intercom telling him the same thing.

"I know, I saw," Lyndquist said, and hurried up to his bubble.

"Which one do you want me to hit first?" Kreuger asked.

"What's the difference... if they attack together we haven't got a chance." He turned to hit the red alert button. An instant later everyone able scurried for the emergency cubicles. "Just hold your fire."

The outsiders now proceeded to shrink their circle as if holding hands. A moment later the sky around them was pitch black punctuated only by twelve sets of yellow eyes. They came within a hundred meters, stopped. Stationery and staring. Glaring...?

After an hour Lyndquist gave up the game and sounded the all clear. As the crewmen came out of their protective cubicles they were stunned—and crying—by what they saw.

Lyndquist came on the intercom. "I don't know what they want out there and I don't know what they plan to do. For the moment they seem to be satisfied with watching us. I don't want anyone to panic. Go about your duties as if everything were back to normal."

Advice easy to give, which no one could follow, and he knew it. There was no porthole on the ship that didn't have a yellow eye looking into it. Understandably, most of the crew was soon busy boarding up the windows. Knowing that they were outside was one thing, seeing their damn eyes was another.

Meanwhile Adam's respirations were becoming labored. There were only a few minutes after the delivery when he'd pinked up, but since then his color had steadily worsened. He'd been checked for infection, and there were no signs of it. His blood tests and chemistries were normal. It was when they took a chest X-ray that they found the answer—it was a "white out," hyaline membrane disease. Before Cortney had awakened from anesthesia the baby was moved to a separate room. His prognosis had gone from serious to critical.

"It can't *be*," she said when she woke. "I know he's okay. I know he'll live...."

"Maybe he can still make it," John said, feeling empty.

"I've got to see him, he's got to know me." She tried sitting up, but the pains in her abdomen stopped her.

And if she'd managed to get up, John would have stopped her. He knew the sight of her baby dying would literally haunt her the rest of her life. He knew that never having seen him alive was better. It hurt him to resist her in this, but it was about time he took some difficult stands. The time for cover-up and well-intentioned dissembling was over.

Over the next twelve hours they continued to wait, and hope, but each time Dr. McLaughlin sent out a report, Adam's condition had worsened. On the fourteenth hour the two physicians asked Dr. Olmschied to join them. No explanation. They just wanted him.

Another hour passed. Olmschied came back. There were undisguised tears in the old man's eyes. Cortney had never seen him cry before. She immediately knew. "My baby's dead, oh, my God, he's dead. . . ." John took her in his arms as the professor nodded confirmation.

As the child's death was announced over the intercom, the skies outside the satellite brightened with starlight.

They had disappeared.

LI

THE FUNERAL service was brief. After Commander Lyndquist read the eulogy and Dr. Olmschied added a few words he could barely get out the wooden cradle was wrapped in a blanket and sent out into space. Cortney watched from a wheelchair. John stood behind her, his hands tightly gripping her shoulders.

Along the outer rim the crew watched from portholes as the tiny casket slowly drifted past. It was their loss too, and many of them felt badly for what they'd wished on him.

The cradle rocked itself along for several minutes, then slowly disappeared from sight.

LII

At Mission Control the news from the Space Lab was received with great excitement. The pressure was finally off. The Space Lab was safe. They'd never known the baby, never really felt the conflict around his life, and death, and were mostly thankful that three thousand men and their billion dollar investment was saved. Of course it was unfortunate for the parents, but apparently it had been the solution for everyone else. And after all, the mother could always have another baby. . . .

There also was suddenly no need for the new shuttles. An old model now easily passed through the earth's atmosphere and sped toward the satellite. It was a smooth, uncomplicated flight carrying emergency food and medical supplies.

Awakened from an exhausted nap in her old room, Cortney could hear them shouting and cheering, but for her the shuttle's arrival was hardly a welcome relief. Long after the ceremony she'd sat at her porthole, hoping—not believing—to get one more look at the casket. She thought of her first instructions with Kreuger and how enthralled she'd been with the various stars. Now she hated them. One of these bright lights out there had no doubt caused Adam's death, sent the agents of it. . . . Now they all shone down as if nothing had changed in the universe had changed. Well, damn them, it had.

John, Cortney and Dr. Olmschied were scheduled to return home on this shuttle's return flight. Although most of the seats had been removed for cargo, Lyndquist was worried about Cortney's health and insisted that they leave first. There was no argument. As far as she was concerned, the sooner the better.

The trip back was a dreary one. No one spoke. It was like riding in a hearse. Even the sky around them was black.

When they docked at Houston and John was wheeling Cortney down the ramp they saw a stretcher coming toward them. Assuming it was for Cortney, he started to tell them it wasn't necessary, but Olmschied interrupted.

"It's not for her... it's for... Adam." The professor tried to sound calm, then directed the attendants to a long blue box that was just being unloaded from the shuttle. Looking at her astonished face, he hurried on... "I'm sorry, but I couldn't tell you. Adam's in Gregor's old back-up crypt. We kept him next to the turbine, where those things were least likely, on account of the noise, you understand, to hear us, and we hoped to buy some time by lowering his temperature. It was the only chance he had."

Cortney couldn't believe what she was hearing. Neither could John... they'd kept it from him too, figuring he was too involved.... Suddenly Cortney's tears were gone. The same crypt that had killed Olmschied's daughter had saved her baby. As they passed her, she could actually see him inside. *Alive....*

The crypt was raced to Children's Hospital, where Adam was slowly warmed and placed on a respirator. Outside the neonatal unit the three waited as the professor explained how he'd begun studying Gregor's techniques once he was certain that toxemia was present. He borrowed mice from another laboratory and added the same shielding that they were using on the laser. None of the creatures seemed to detect what was going on, or at least none of them interfered, and when the time came, he took the gamble. He hated to do it to Cortney, but if he'd let her in on the secret those things might have discovered it somehow through her. They had certainly seemed fine-tuned to her, to the baby....

The baby's struggle to live, though, was not over. He was still seriously ill, severely dehydrated and very lethargic. His lungs were severely congested with the hyaline disease, and for a while it looked as though every heartbeat might be his last.

The hours waiting carried into days, and the three of

them continued their vigil. Cortney felt she couldn't take it again. That cradle floating in space was still too fresh in her mind. She loved the professor for what he'd done, it just couldn't be for nothing.

On the third night the doctors thought that Adam might be improving. By morning it was definite. His oxygen requirements leveled off at fifty percent, then slowly returned to normal. Even the X-ray showed clearing. Finally they could change his listed condition from grave to serious, and then to fair.

It took them an additional two days to wean Adam from the respirator and started on feedings. Every minute that they'd allow her, Cortney was inside attending him. He was the smallest baby that she'd ever seen, blue eyes, blond hair. Who cared about that. He was beautiful because he was alive.

On the sixth day she was allowed to pick him up. It was the first time she'd felt him outside her own body. He squirmed in her arms, seemed, she decided, to recognize his mother.

During this period Adam's presence in Children's Hospital was kept a secret from the world. Government officials, in particular Dr. Leigh, were concerned that the intruders—the irony of that designation for them escaped him—might come back if they ever learned that they'd been deceived.

"My family has a farm in southern Illinois. We can keep him there," John told them. Cortney had already agreed.

The Space Commissioner thought for a moment before answering. "I don't know, it could still be risky. I had something more in mind . . . change in name and total relocation. We should try to erase every bit of your background and start you all over again."

"We'll do anything," Cortney said quickly, and John nodded agreement. "Anything to be sure this baby lives."

•   •   •

Meanwhile, just beyond the walls inside the nursery, the baby was echoing the conversation... "I don't know, it could still be risky. I had something more in mind... a change in name and total relocation. We should try to erase every bit of your background and start you all over again.... We'll do anything. Anything to be sure this baby lives."... Word for word, inflection for inflection.

And somewhere out in space those exact same words were being echoed again, and again, and again.

To be continued....

New Bestsellers from Berkley...
The best in paperback reading!

___BY THE RIVERS OF
BABYLON   (04431-9—$2.75)
Nelson De Mille

___THE LAST CONVERTIBLE   (04034-8—$2.50)
Anton Myrer

___THE LEGACY   (04183-2—$2.25)
John Coyne, based on a story
by Jimmy Sangster

___LINKS   (04048-8—$2.25)
Charles Panati

___LEAH'S JOURNEY   (04430-0—$2.50)
Gloria Goldreich

___NURSE   (04220-0—$2.50)
Peggy Anderson

___STAR SIGNS FOR LOVERS   (04238-3—$2.50)
Robert Worth

___THE TANGENT FACTOR   (04120-4—$2.25)
Lawrence Sanders

___A TIME FOR TRUTH   (04185-9—$2.50)
William E. Simon

___THE VISITOR   (04210-3—$2.50)
Jere Cunningham

Available at your local bookstore or return this form to:

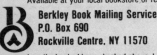

**Berkley Book Mailing Service
P.O. Box 690
Rockville Centre, NY 11570**

Please send me the books I have checked above. I am enclosing $_____ (please
add 50¢ to cover postage and handling).
Send check or money order—no cash or C.O.D.'s please.

Name_____

Address_____

City_____ State/Zip_____

Please allow three weeks for delivery.   1

You have nothing to fear.
It doesn't want you…
It wants your child!

THE VISITOR
JERE CUNNINGHAM

It escapes, screaming from the hidden, tortured world of the exclusive sanitarium known as Rosewood. It glides like a shadow from Hell through the walls of a young woman's new home, in search of a spirit as lost as its own.

It wants her child…her only son.

In her desperate struggle to save him, she is plunged into a waking nightmare. She waits helplessly for the unknown force, chilled with the ancient memory of an unspeakable evil.

A Berkley Paperback $2.50